WAKEN, LORDS AND LADIES GAY

Selected Stories of Desmond Pacey

THE CANADIAN SHORT STORY LIBRARY

Glenn Clever, General Editor.

Editorial Board:

Austen Clarke
Marian Engel
Hugh Hood
John Metcalfe
W. O. Mitchell
Alden Nowlan
Leo Simpson

WAKEN, LORDS AND LADIES GAY

Selected Stories of Desmond Pacey

Edited and With an Introduction
by
FRANK M. TIERNEY

UNIVERSITY OF OTTAWA PRESS
OTTAWA, CANADA
1974

Printed and bound in Canada.

All rights reserved: The University of Ottawa Press, 1974
ISBN-0-7766-4334-7

TABLE OF CONTENTS

Introduction	9
Waken, Lords and Ladies Gay	17
The Picnic	29
The Boat	37
That Day in the Bush	45
When She Comes Over	51
On The Roman Road	57
The Test	65
The Mirror	75
The Trespasser	81
Aunt Polly	87
The Ghost of Reddleman Lane	95
The Lost Girl	101
Bibliography	109

Introduction

Desmond Pacey's reputation as a major figure in Canadian Literature has been long established. He is an outstanding scholar, a leader in University education and a significant creative artist. His works *Frederick Philip Grove* (1945), *Creative Writing in Canada* (1952), and *Ten Canadian Poets* (1957), to mention only a few, have had leadership impact on Canadian scholarship. Gratitude for his contribution is evidenced by the many honours he has received. Among them was his election to the Royal Society of Canada in 1955; he won the Lorne Pierce Medal in 1972.

His leadership has been significant at the University of New Brunswick as well. During his career there he has served as Professor of English Literature, Chairman of the Department of English and Dean of Graduate Studies, and at present is Acting President of the University. One could expect that this demanding work would afford little opportunity for creative writing. Fortunately for Canadian letters Professor Pacey has found time to write and publish thirty-one delightful short stories to date, twelve of which have been selected for this series.

It was, frankly, difficult to make a selection. It was, in fact, with regret that a selection had to be made. All of his stories are worthy of reappearance in print.

Of his thirty-one short stories sixteen were published in his book *The Picnic and Other Stories* (1958). The remaining nineteen have appeared in various Canadian journals and magazines. His short stories have been translated into German and Swiss, and many have been broadcast by the Canadian Broadcasting Corporation programme *Canadian Short Stories*.

The twelve stories that follow are typical of his story-telling technique. Professor Roy Daniells, in his valuable "Foreward" to *The Picnic And Other Stories*, observes:

> Each of [these stories] recounts a brief excursion along the road of experience, the events being related in the order of their occurrence without benefit of flash-back, montage or even stream-of-consciousness. This immemorial method of story-telling now strikes us as an innovation, calculated to restore the objective world to us. At least, we say to ourselves, this is an account of things as they actually happened. Disbelief is the more easily suspended because today a straight-forward tale again seems more natural than a telescoping of time or a plunge toward the unconscious.

This naturalism reinforces the presentation of uncomplicated characters in simple, usually rural, settings. Professor Pacey's technique presents the real recognizable world and an account of things as they actually happen.

There are essentially two worlds in which these stories are set: seven take place in rural Canada and five in England. But even the English settings are predominantly rural. There are none of the usual urban complexities that mark contemporary literature. Professor Pacey's simple country settings contain a purity and freshness which he describes in a warm, humane tone. Clearly, he writes from deep personal experience. In a recent letter concerning "Waken Lords and Ladies Gay" Professor Pacey wrote "one of the chief purposes of all my stories is to bring back to life characters I have known". The result is a realism upon which his imagination works confidently and artistically to a smooth and pleasing finale.

In the opening lines of "The Picnic" the joy and excitement experienced by the family enroute to a picnic is supported by the harmony of nature and tranquil beauty of sky, river and trees:

> The sky was a soft blue dotted here and there with wispy white clouds like puffs of floating smoke; the surface of the river was just barely disturbed by a faint spring breeze; the trees on either side of the highway gently ruffled their new leaves like pigeons preening their feathers in the sun.

The mood of the family and the mood of nature blend in simple harmony. This blend is revealed explicitly in characters who, in their uncomplicated personalities, manifest openness, love, creativity, and values that are obviously lacking in those who are egocentric. These values are found, for example, in the boy narrator in "Waken, Lords and Ladies Gay"; the boy Gerald in "The Boat"; and the boy in "That Day in the Bush". But these qualities are not limited to children. They are potential in all humanity. So Tom, in "The Boat", while struggling with personal frustrations is able to express a high degree of awareness and love. These qualities are not suppressed by his lack of material goods, his sense of insecurity, and his ill health. It is interesting that characters with positive attitudes are set, generally, in humble circumstances.

Another character who fits into this positive frame of reference is Polly in "Aunt Polly". She too, like Tom, is concerned about people: "But Aunt Polly now — there is a woman one can only love... she was the very soul of kindness and gaiety. Just to look at her was enough to make one's spirits expand". And the narrator describes her appearance and attitude:

> But to be afraid of Aunt Polly was out of the question. She had a round face, a ruddy complexion usually rendered more striking by the heat from the oven (for she was always baking the most delicious pies and cakes a boy ever tasted), full but not thick lips which stretched into a smile on the slightest occasion, and bright blue eyes which looked out on the world with complete confidence.

Aunt Polly is enlightened.

An obvious juxtaposition to Aunt Polly is Mrs. Cooper in "The Trespasser". She is restricted and cramped by artificiality and hypocrisy. Her *house*, in contrast to Aunt Polly's *home*, is well ordered, efficient and cold. George, the boy who has been manipulated by Mrs. Cooper:

> dashed out of the front door and began to run down the driveway. His feet crunched loudly in the gravel, disturbing the still-silent garden. But now the garden had an evil, menacing silence; the shrubs were dark and twisted shapes; the trees crouched like savage beasts.

Again, imagery reinforces the moods of the characters. And it is interesting, too, that a boy is also juxtaposed against Mrs. Cooper. His response to her is revulsion.

But perhaps the supreme character, the one who demonstrates potential continuity of love actualized in old age, is the old man in "The Lost Girl". He is a symbol of responsibility and charity. This is the last story in *The Picnic And Other Stories*. Perhaps, too, it is the most beautiful. It is the summation of the eternal opposing forces of good and evil in the world. The narrator describes the old man as an individual "who caught the eye" among the masses on the ocean beach. He is curious, aware, attentive, responsible. Because of love he is willing to risk ridicule and condemnation. And the background is striking. The old man, who is the epitome of Christian action, (not in a narrow religious sense, but more general, more mysterious, more existential), is seen against the perpetually cleansing and uniquely rejuvenating power of the sea. This power is analagous to the power of love.

Again in "The Picnic", as the family continues its pleasant drive, the narrator observes: "The land across the river was dotted with white and yellow farmhouses and their huddled grey barns; here and there you could see farmers on tractors or behind teams of horses rhythmically moving back and forth across the fields as they did the spring seeding." The family in the car *sees* the trees ruffling their leaves, *sees* the tractor in the distance "rhythmically moving back and forth". The picture is purified of disturbing and distracting sounds. Through his personal experience and aesthetic sensibility, Professor Pacey expresses that moment of beauty which has at its center silence, tranquility, and peace. This center is the condition, perhaps the only condition, for real self awareness, real self identity, and real communion with the ultimate reality. It is, surely, that condition of detachment from artificialities of society that permits an epiphany and the center also from which meditation is possible. Several of his characters are at this center.

Desmond Pacey writes from deep experience of farm life. Consequently, the settings are real and meaningful. In "The Boat", a simple precise description produces a typical farm atmosphere:

> They came to the machine-shed, and the man pulled back the heavy sliding door. Inside it was cool and dark and the air smelt of oil and old leather and rusty iron. On the packed earth floor, between drill and mower and other out-of-season implements, were tins of nails, boxes of nuts and scraps of broken harness, scattered pieces of wood left from various repair jobs.

The setting for "The Mirror" is a "small, raw Western Canadian town". "The Trespasser" takes place in a minister's home which appears "grander, statelier that he [Gerald] imagined... All was order, innocence, peace;" This apparently tranquil middle class urbane setting contains a sophisticated civilized person whose aim is ridicule and whose character is hypocritical.

But urbanity is seldom used in Professor Pacey's stories. And where it is found it is usually accompanied, as in "The Trespasser", by hypocrisy. Simple, even primitive settings, contain the most admirable characters. None of the stories has a complex urban background. Six have country settings, one has a rural school house, and five take place in small rural towns. Within this general simplicity there is great variety of subject matter and tone. For example, "When She Comes Over", one of the Cambridge group, is a delightful and humorous story about a young student waiting for his fiancée to come to Cambridge so that they can get married. While waiting he is entangled with his young attractive landlady. The result is charming and amusing.

The story "That Day in the Bush" is an example of Professor Pacey's rural Ontario stories. Again, his supreme achievement with mood can be attributed, in part, to his experience as a boy living in rural Ontario, but more important to his deep sensitivity to the beauty of nature. He is, of course, first and foremost a skillful artist. He has the precision and polish of the poet who can present a delightful picture of reality in a few words. But pictures never are an end in themselves. They are landscapes used through a magical formula to produce a mood and precise psychic state in the reader. Two brief examples reveal his technique. The first is an authentic experience of a young farm boy rising at dawn and dressing for work. This is a typical Ontario farm in the first third of the twentieth Century. The fire in the woodstove is permitted to die out during the night. It is winter. The house is cold. The first person awake in the morning must light the woodstove:

> He dressed quickly in his overalls, workshirt and sweater, and went downstairs. His father had already lit the kitchen stove and the boy sat close to it as he put on his shoes. Then, slipping on his cap and mackinaw coat, he went out to the barn.
>
> The barn was warm and moist with the breath of horses and cattle, and full of a predominantly pleasant odour made up of the mingled scents of hay, ensilage, and straw.

The authenticity of the experience captivates the reader.

The second is the silent beauty of an early winter morning landscape:

> The air was crisp and clear, there was no wind, and the temperature was well above zero. The snow was fresh but not deep enough to be a nuisance: about two inches had fallen in the night and made a loose brilliant covering over the three or four inches of more closely-packed old snow beneath.

> The youth and the man trudged silently down the lane, each deep in his own thoughts. It seemed to the boy that the farm had never looked so beautiful. The branches of the hickory, maple, and elm trees beside the lane and along the fences in the fields were powdered with the light snow. The dark grey barns of the next farm stood out in vivid outline against the white background of the surrounding fields. Here and there were clumps of bush, a dull blue-grey against the brighter and lighter blue of the sky.

Plots are uncomplicated. They usually deal with external events and simple realistic situations. In "Waken, Lords and Ladies Gay" the plot develops around the experience of two boys with three teachers and the boys' reactions to school. Tension and suspense are well used to highten the pleasure. What is the future for these teachers? Who is the stranger disturbing Mrs. Newcome and her child?

Professor Daniells rightly places Desmond Pacey's stories in the tradition of Canadian short story writers:

> Such naturalness and such reliance upon straight-forward narrative have always been typical of the Canadian short-story. Early stories in the *Literary Garland* were anecdotal and concerned with the deeds of frontier and rural character-types. In the middle of the last century the best writers, including D.C. Scott and Stephen Leacock, avoided complexity of fiction pattern. After the First Great War, when the techniques of the new realism had become almost traditional in Europe and America, Canadian story writers preferred older and more romantic forms. Among the best Canadian stories written just before and during the Second Great War are those of Sinclair Ross and they rely upon perfectly straight forward narrative. It is of interest that his reading of the work of Ross, in Winnipeg during the winter of 1940-41, stirred Desmond Pacey to renew an interest in writing short-stories, for the first time since his undergraduate days in Victoria College.

The influence of Katherine Mansfield on Professor Pacey's style and themes is highlighted by Professor Daniells. "The Trespasser" is an illustration. Gerald, the unsuspecting open boy, is "wounded in the house of his apparent friends." The element of death in many of these stories is another indication of Mansfield's influence.

But none of the stories dwells on death. Nor are they concerned with lust and violence. Although death is an ingredient, it is the effect of death on those remaining that is usually explored. Their responses reveal their characters.

These stories contain the philosophy of "wonder" of, for example, John Ruskin. The adult world contains many people who have "eyes but cannot see". By inordinate attachment to worldly things they have blinded themselves to truth and beauty. Nine of the stories have children as important characters. In six of the nine, the events are seen through the eyes of a boy. The result is a juxtaposition of the boy's sense of wonder with the spiritual corrusion of adults. The boys are not uninterested in the world around them. They are vitally concerned. But they have a healthy flexibility and adaptability and a natural mysterious power to perceive truth; a truth that is hidden from most adults by their passionate attachment to the things of the world. The world of grown-ups, therefore, is frequently a world of frustration, selfishness and pain. It is a world that, most often, has lost its youthful spontaneity and joy.

This sense of wonder is obvious in the boy narrator in "Waken, Lords and Ladies Gay", and in the young Ontario farm boy in "That Day in the Bush". Their attitudes of detachment permit a wide view of the universe. This view is frequently expressed with a pictorial quality (for example, see "The Picnic" discussed above), which is reminiscent of the PreRaphaelite Brotherhood.

What emerges from this group of stories, then, is a distinctive, even powerful optimism, charity, tolerance and deep understanding of human nature. The sombre side of life is honestly portrayed and juxtaposed against the importance of love as a unifying force. These stories, presented in a simple straightforward manner, reveal man as he is: fragile, vulnerable, capable of crude, selfish and irrational behaviour, subject to defeat and despair; but also, heroic, enlightened, capable of strength, wisdom, hope and joy. Let us wish and hope, then, that Professor Pacey's duties will allow time for more stories so that we can continue to share in his joyful creative experiences and his enlightened view of life.

Waken, Lords and Ladies Gay

Miss Breakspear, as her name suggests, was stern and strict, but she didn't look nearly as tough as she was. Even to my eight-year-old eyes she seemed tiny, fragile, and delicate. She can't have been more than five feet two inches tall, her weight was probably about seven stones or ninety-eight pounds at most, and she wore dark grey or dark brown "costumes" that came down almost to her ankles. Her face was almost a dead white and was thickly wrinkled, and it contrasted strongly with her bright red hair. Looking back, I know the hair must have been a wig, but it didn't occur to me at the time. The most striking thing about her looks, however, was not the red wig, but her eyes — they were very dark and really "beady", like the eyes on a stuffed toy tiger. Those eyes looked right through you, but you couldn't look through them at all. I suppose she wasn't much more than fifty-five years old, but to us boys she seemed ancient.

No one took any liberties with Miss Breakspear. Not even Archie Leatherhead. Archie was the son of the keeper of the village pub, the King Charles' Head, and definitely the toughest kid of his age in the school. He was one of those stocky, cocky boys who grow up to be professional football players or professional soldiers or professional crooks. Already, at eight, he had a stock of swear-words which would have shocked even a sergeant-major.

And Archie had a disposition that matched his language. He loved a fight, and he'd take on anybody. The oldest boys in the village school were fourteen, and Archie would just as soon fight one of them as someone his own age like me. Actually I never gave him a chance to fight me — and I didn't try to justify my reluctance by arguing that discretion was the better part of valour or any muck like that either. I just didn't fancy getting beaten up by such a tough little bastard, so I went along with him. When he cracked a joke, I laughed. It was as simple as that.

But I guess that even Archie knew that he had met his match in Miss Breakspear, for he never gave her any sauce. And she in turn must have admired his mettle, for she never picked on him. It was meek little me she went for, day in and day out.

You see her name was suggestive not only because it made you think of battles and tournaments and knights and things but because it made you think of Shakespeare and plays and poetry and all that stuff — and Miss Breakspear really did have a thing about poetry. She had a well-thumbed copy of Palgrave's *Golden Treasury* and whenever things were getting a bit dull with the old arithmetic or the Kings of England and all their dates and battles she'd read us one of the poems.

A reading by Miss Breakspear was something to remember. She'd rear back on those short little legs of hers, fix her beady eyes on the book, and really let it rip. She had a voice that was amazing for a woman so small: when she started to recite people must have been able to hear her all over the village.

> Waken, Lords and Ladies Gay,
> On the Mountain dawns the day...

she'd start, and if anyone of us in the big schoolroom was having a nap we snapped out of it in a hurry. And if the poem was of another sort, she could put on a kind of creepy, crepey voice that would bring out a crop of goosepimples even on Archie Leatherhead:

> I saw wherein the shroud did lurk
> A curious frame of nature's work;
> A flow'ret crushéd in the bud,
> A nameless piece of babyhood,
> Was in her cradle-coffin lying ...

After one of her poems like that I'd lie awake all night in the little bedroom at my grandmother's, turning on the flashlight I kept under my pillow to make sure that the creaking noises I was hearing were coming from the old apple tree outside my window and not from some ghostly visitor indoors.

But Miss Breakspear had a third style of reading — Archie called it her whisper-voice, and behind her back he'd make fun of it though to her face he'd be as serious and hushed as the rest of us. She used her whisper-voice on poems like "The Death Bed". She knew several such poems by heart, so she'd close the *Treasury* and lay it on the desk behind her, clasp her hands in front of her thin bosom, close her eyes, tilt her head towards the ceiling, and then just barely breathe the words so that we all had to strain to hear her:

>We watch'd her breathing thro' the night,
>Her breathing soft and low,
>As in her breast the wave of life
>Kept heaving to and fro.
>So silently we seemed to speak,
>So slowly moved about,
>As we had lent her half our powers
>To eke her living out.

Now if Miss Breakspear had been content to recite these poems herself, none of us would have minded. Of course we had to pretend to find the whole stunt silly, and say things to Archie like "Wasn't the old cow awful today? When she read that poem about that damn dying baby I thought I would have to puke!", but secretly we all found the readings quite thrilling, and certainly a hell of a lot better than trying to remember the dates of Ethelred the Unready or to find the square root of a hundred and twenty-one.

The trouble was that Miss Breakspear insisted on *us* learning the poems by heart, and then reciting them ourselves to the school. Now I was already very fond of poetry, though I would never have admitted it to Archie, but I was also already aware of a weakness that I have never managed to overcome: I can't memorize poems exactly word for word. Archie, on the other hand, said — and I believe he meant it — that poetry was for young girls and old women, but he had a photographic memory, and having read a poem once he could spout it off without any bother at all. Instead of letting Archie show off, however, nine times out of ten Miss B. would call on me to recite. I'd stagger to my feet, Archie poking a pencil into my back as I did so, and in a choked voice begin:

>I remember, I remember
>The house where I was born ...

only to realize once more that I didn't remember at all. Was it a "little window" or "a narrow window" where the sun came creeping (peeping? peering? glinting?) in at morn or dawn?

For such stupidity Miss Breakspear had no mercy. The moment I began to stumble she would dig the sharp point of her pencil into my skull and say something like "Don't you know you're ruining a beautiful poem? Whoever heard of a sun *creeping*? *Peeping*, you idiot. *Peeping, peeping, peeping!*" — and with each "peeping" she'd dig that pencil in again until it felt just like being crucified with a crown of thorns.

So I wasn't too sorry when, at the end of that year, Miss Breakspear resigned in order to go and live with her recently widowed older sister in a cottage in Appleby in County Westmoreland. I sadly missed *her* readings, but I was happy to miss mine.

The new teacher was Mr. Jagger, who lived up to his name by having a jagged face and an explosive temper. His face was jagged because he had had half of it shot away in the War, and the whole of one side of it was a livid mess. He was pretty terrifying to look at at first, but after a while we all got used to his face and hardly noticed it. Apart from his scarred face, his appearance was not particularly outstanding. Although he had risen through the ranks from private to corporal to sergeant to lieutenant he was a small man, only about five feet six in height and ten stones in weight, and it was hard to imagine him giving orders on a parade ground or anywhere else.

To be fair to him, Jagger didn't boast much about his military exploits, though he had won the Military Medal and later the Military Cross. When he told us stories about the War, as he often did, he played down his own part in it. He told us, for example, how he got his various promotions, and in each case, according to his version of the affair, it was more accident than good management. I remember he told us he became a sergeant, for example, because an officer noticed he had a loud voice.

Mr. Jagger's war stories played the role in his régime that Miss Breakspear's poetry readings did in hers. When the long afternoons were dragging on interminably through the mazes of English history, Archie or I would find some excuse to ask Jagger what the war in the trenches was really like, and soon he'd be off on reminiscences of mud and rats and German corpses and howitzers flying overhead and barbed wire entanglements and so on. I daresay the girls were bored or shocked by it all, but Archie and I and the other boys lapped it up and hoped that we would always have a male teacher and not another of those fussy old women.

Most of the time things went smoothly enough under Mr. Jagger. For an old soldier he seemed remarkably good-tempered, and even Archie Leatherhead seemed to have a sneaking respect for him. One day, however, we discovered that Mr. Jagger did have a truly ferocious temper when it was aroused.

Archie had a knack for drawing, and being Archie he wasn't satisfied to draw the flowers and cones and cubes and wall-paper patterns that we were assigned to draw in class. In fact there was really only one thing that Archie liked to draw, and that was the female form. For a boy of nine he had a quite staggering familiarity with female anatomy, a familiarity which was rumoured to spring from his relationship with his fourteen year old sister, a sexy blonde who already had quite a reputation throughout the village and beyond. Wherever his knowledge came from, Archie certainly had it and liked to display it.

This particular day I was clumsily trying to get something down on paper that would look faintly like the vase of snapdragons that Mr. Jagger had set up as a model — I was no better at drawing than at memorizing poetry, in fact I was worse — when I felt Archie's pencil digging into my shoulder. I half turned round, and he furtively pushed a folded piece of paper into my hand. I crumpled it up into a ball, shoved it under the lid of my desk, and kept my eye out for a suitable moment to look at it. My chance came a few minutes later, when Mr. Jagger was leaning over Archie's sister's shoulder and looking closely either at her drawing or down her bosom — I couldn't tell which, but it was a bit of both, most likely; after all, old Jagger was only about thirty-five, and the Leatherhead girl had a bust many a twenty year old would have envied. Even at nine I used to dream about it.

Well, maybe my suspicions of old Jagger's intentions were coloured by what I expected to find in Archie's drawing — and when I did take a gander at it I certainly wasn't disappointed. If this was what his sister looked like when she stripped for bed at night, I didn't blame him for "peeping" like the sun.

I was daydreaming about doing a little peeping into that little old window myself some morning when an iron grip suddenly seized my shoulder and Jagger's other hand snatched the drawing from my fingers. "Hunt," he said, in the voice he must have used when he was a sergeant on parade, "What in God's name do you think you're doing?"

"I'm drawing, sir," I said, trying to divert his attention by pointing to my pathetic attempt at a bowl of snapdragons.

"Of course you're drawing! Did you draw this?" He held the bosomy sketch close in front of my eyes.

"No sir."

"Then where," and with this he began to cuff me alternately with his right hand and his left, "where" smack "did" smack "you" smack "get" smack "this" smack "obscene" smack "thing" smack? Well, I'd been thinking of putting my hand up to go to the toilet just about the very minute Archie first prodded me, and the sudden and very noticeable effect of all this pounding was that the old bladder let go and a pool began to gather on the floor below my desk. This weakness on my part seemed to activate Archie's conscience, because he said, "It's my drawing, sir. I did it."

Old Jagger's anger had seemed to be subsiding as the tell-tale pool spread to his feet, but now his temper rose again in full fury and he started to pound Archie on the back.

"You dirty, sneaking, filthy toad, you," he said, "I'll teach you to draw dirty pictures in my school!"

And then a terrible thing happened — Archie got his temper up and started to fight back! It just seemed as if the whole world were about to come to an end — a pupil actually fighting a teacher! Archie got his foot out and tripped Jagger and fell on top of him, and then Jagger twisted free and got on top of Archie and started pummelling his head up and down against the floor. One of the girls started a rush for the door, and in no time at all we were all out of there and on our way home.

I don't know how Archie and Jagger patched it up, but they must have managed somehow for they were both back to normal the next day.

But it wouldn't be fair to end my account of Jagger on this note, for this was the only time he really lost his temper. Perhaps because he wanted to make it up to Archie, who was the best footballer in the school even when he was nine, going on ten, Jagger decided that we should get up a school team to go and play his old school in Barnsley. That may sound easy, but when you realize that we only had twenty boys in the whole school, varying in age from five to fourteen, and that the Barnsley school had about twelve forms with thirty or forty boys in each, you'll see that it was a David and Goliath operation if there ever was one.

The prospect of the trip to Barnsley changed the whole pattern of school life. Instead of arriving at about one minute to nine, reluctant to enter prison a second earlier than necessary, the fifteen boys who had a chance of making the team would arrive every morning at eight-thirty, and practise like mad under Jagger's supervision until the bell rang. At the mid-morning break we'd go at it again. At noontime we'd gobble our sandwiches and have another session. After school, we stayed for an hour each day and practised some more. Jagger had played soccer for his regiment, so he made a good coach: we quickly learned something about the game.

The girls got into the act too. It had been agreed that Jagger would charter a bus for the trip, and the bus was to hold thirty-five passengers — nearly every boy and girl in the school. To pay for the bus, the girls baked cakes and biscuits — or got their mothers to — and had food sales in the schoolyard at weekends. And one evening we put on, for the entertainment of the villagers, what was billed as an operetta. It was a "musical" version of *Little Red Riding Hood*, and Archie played the wolf, his sister Gladys the girl, Mr. Jagger the grandmother, and I the woodsman. Captain Oates, the chairman of the local school board, was the master of ceremonies, and that really lent tone to the affair. Everybody came. The whole show must have been lousy, however, for I forgot the words in the middle of my big song, and afterwards my Uncle Billy, never one to flatter, told me that whatever else I could do, I certainly couldn't sing. The show had two good features, though: we took in enough money to pay over half the bus-hire and I got to kiss the bosomy Gladys — after all, I'd saved her from the wicked wolf!

At last the great day dawned, and the thirty-five of us set off for Barnsley at eight in the morning. By ten o'clock we boys were changed and ready for the game. We must have looked like an odd crew, for we were of all ages and sizes, whereas the Barnsley team were all fourteen-year-olds and had played together for two or three years. We had to borrow a set of their old jerseys, and on the nine-year-olds, such as Archie and me, they reached almost to our knees! Anyway, odd-looking or not, we lined up, Archie at centre-forward and me at left-half, and the whistle blew. I must say, Archie's sister and the other girls gave us a tremendous cheer, and old Jagger looked proud enough to burst.

Of course at this point I'm tempted to twist the truth and tell you that all the practising paid off and that we won the game against all odds. I guess, however, I'd better be honest and admit that it was clearly a mismatch and that we lost. We lost — but not without honour. With about one minute to go we were down seven goals to nil. A Barnsley player had just shot wide, and our goalkeeper lofted his best kick of the day right to me. More by luck than cunning I trapped the ball, tapped it ahead to the left winger, and followed up. The winger slipped a pass back inside to me; and as I took it I saw out of the corner of my eye old Archie sneak past their centre-half. I got the ball over to Archie, he squeezed between the two full-backs, and ping! the old ball was in the net! Well, the way Mr. Jagger hugged Archie after that you'd never believe they'd had that fight over a drawing.

After all the excitement of the Barnsley trip it was a real letdown when Mr. Jagger told us next summer that he was moving to a bigger school just outside Nottingham. The third teacher, Mrs. Newcome, started under quite a handicap — but fortunately she had a few things going for her, too.

Mrs. Newcome was not a fussy old woman like Miss Breakspear but a very attractive young woman. She had light blonde hair that hung almost to her shoulders, blue eyes that were very appealing, a bosom that didn't fall too far short of Gladys' standard, and legs that were slim and very shapely in their sheer silk stockings under a short skirt.

The big mystery, of course, was how come she was *Mrs.* Newcome, and had a little boy of three, for there was no husband in evidence and she didn't look more than twenty-five. At first we all took her to be a widow, but pretty soon the rumour got around that she was "divorced", a word that in those days suggested something really wicked, if not downright evil.

Archie Leatherhead went for Mrs. Newcome in a big way. We were now ten going on for eleven and the juices were definitely starting to flow. With me the chief effect was that I started reading sexy novels from the village library by the light of my flashlamp under the sheets at night — novels by people like Hall Caine and Marie Corelli in which beauteous dames strip off their clothes beside a fireplace because they've been soaked in the rain or something, and stand there in front of some handsome man, their "magnificent flanks warmed by the glow of the fire" and so on and so forth.

All that was close enough to the reality of sex for my timid self, but Archie, no doubt spurred on by his sister, believed in more direct action. He started to flirt with Mrs. Newcome: he'd give her the old eye, and when he came to such lines in *The Golden Treasury* as

> This is the morn should bring unto this grove
> My Love, to hear and recompense my love.

he'd look soulfully right into her eyes and then make a kissing motion with his lips or wink at her.

To keep a closer watch on Archie's mischief, Mrs. Newcome made him and me change places, and thus had him in the desk right in front of her big teacher's desk. I really think she was a bit flattered by his attention, however.

Now Mrs. Newcome wasn't as tough as Miss Breakspear or Mr. Jagger in some ways — if I stumbled while reciting a poem, for example, she'd encourage me rather than dig in the point of the pencil — but there were some thing she wouldn't stand for. One of these was being late for school. After the flurry of the early football practices, we boys had slipped into the bad old way of trying to get to school as near to nine o'clock as possible, and quite often this turned out to be a few minutes after rather than a few minutes before. For a while Mrs. Newcome tried shaming us into coming early by merely reproaching us and starting at us sadly out of her big blue eyes, but when that didn't work she bought herself a cane and decreed that for every minute we were late we'd get one stroke of the weapon. Archie and I were the chief recipients of these blows, and if she happened to catch us right at the end of the fingers with that swift downward swish it really stung.

There came the day when Archie went too far. He'd arrived five minutes late and taken the five swishes on his hand, and whether this had stirred him up or what I don't know — but I do know, because I could see it from my seat right behind him, that when Mrs. Newcome was bending over his desk beside him correcting his arithmetic homework he started to slip his hand up between her silky legs.

He'd barely started when she straightened up fast, blushing, and said "Leatherhead! How dare you? Come to the front and be caned!"

Archie must have figured that five strokes in one morning were enough, for he just sat in his seat and glared at her. She started towards him as if she were going to pull him out of the desk, but he picked up his pen and made as if he were going to stab her with it if she came an inch closer. They stayed glaring at one another like that for a minute or two, and then Mrs. Newcome started to cry and went out into the little teacher's room where there was a telephone.

She came back in a few minutes, not crying any longer but looking horribly pale and drawn, and said in a thin, strained voice, "I have called Captain Oates, and he will deal with you, Leatherhead."

Captain Oates was a big, burly ex-Army officer who was the closest thing the village had to a squire. He had a big farm on the outskirts of the village, and we kids would see him in his heavy tweeds striding over his fields with a gun, watching for rabbits or hares or pheasants to shoot. We were all scared stiff of him, for he was rumoured to have a horrible temper, and his red face, bristly moustache and bushy eyebrows seemed to confirm the rumour. He also had the D.S.O. (which we boys translated as "doodle shot off") so he must have been very brave.

You might have expected Archie to run away or something, but he must have realized himself that he had gone too far this time, for he just sat at his desk with a hangdog expression on his face and waited. The school clock ticked like a tick of doom while we waited for the Captain — the first time I had ever noticed it.

Eventually Captain Oates arrived, whispered with Mrs. Newcome for a few seconds, and then in a loud, harsh voice said, "Leatherhead! You are a disgrace to this school and this village. Come forward and take your punishment." He picked up the cane.

Archie shambled forward.

"Hold out your right hand!"

Archie held out his right hand, and was given ten mighty strokes, wincing more noticeably each time but not crying out. Each time the cane connected I could feel the shock running right through my own hands, and they were wet with sweat.

"Hold out your left hand!"

Again the ten strokes, with us all wincing in sympathy. I couldn't even look.

"Now resume your desk, and don't let me ever hear of such disgraceful conduct on your part again", and with a curt, lordly nod to the class, and a slow bow to Mrs. Newcome, Captain Oates left.

I'll say this for Archie, he sure had guts. He didn't cry over the beating, or even complain about it, but was merely very quiet for the rest of that day and a little more quiet than usual for the rest of the week. I thought he had it in for her, though, and expected a new outbreak any day.

Then things started happening to Mrs. Newcome. One morning on my way past her house to school I noticed a ladder leaning against an upstairs window, and when Mrs. Newcome arrived at school, late herself for the first time ever, she looked terribly pale and anxious and was all red around the eyes. Moreover, she had her little boy with her. Up to now she had left the boy at home in the charge of one of the fifteen year old village girls who had finished school, but every day from now on she brought him to school and had him sit on a little chair beside her desk, doing some colouring or looking at a picture-book.

Soon the rumour spread throughout the village that Mrs. Newcome's sailor husband had come back from sea, and that he was the one who had put the ladder against her window and tried to break in. There were two theories about all this — one was that the husband was anxious to get back with her, and she wouldn't have him, and the other that he was after the little boy. It was all very mysterious and exciting.

One morning we were in the middle of doing a geography lesson when the door was roughly pushed open and in came a man in the uniform of a petty officer of the merchant marine. Mrs. Newcome gasped "Oh my God", dropped the geography book and grabbed the little boy. The man made straight for her, and started to pull the boy away from her.

We all sat in stunned silence for a few seconds, and then, "Come on, Hunt and you other guys", yelled Archie, and made a dive for the man's legs. About six of us footballers joined him, and in a few seconds we had the guy pinned to the floor beneath us.

"Good for you, Archie," said Mrs. Newcome, "I'll call Captain Oates."

Captain Oates was there in no time, and as he had some kind of special police permit or something he was able to put the fellow under arrest and take him away.

Things settled down after that. I had to write the county scholarship examinations that spring to qualify for entrance to Grammar School the next year, so I started to hit the books in a big way and didn't pay too much attention to anything else. By September Mrs. Newcome had left for a destination unknown, I was going by bus every day to the Grammar School in the nearest large town, and Archie was breaking in a fourth teacher.

The Picnic

I started the car and began to back out of the driveway. As usual, I had to tell the kids to sit down in the back seat so that I could see if there was anything coming. As it was, I just stopped in time to miss a delivery truck which was speeding up the street.

Within five minutes we were out of the city and scudding along the river road. What a day for our first picnic of the season, for our very first picnic since moving to this new district! The sky was a soft blue dotted here and there with wispy white clouds like puffs of floating smoke; the surface of the river was just barely disturbed by a faint spring breeze; the trees on either side of the highway gently ruffled their new leaves like pigeons preening their feathers in the sun.

"Is everybody happy?" I called out.

"We are!" came the answering duet from the kids behind me.

"What about Mummy?" In sheer exuberance I patted Edith's knee beside me.

"Fine and dandy!" she said, but she pushed my hand away. "Don't be taking chances," she went on. "You don't know this road, and it seems to twist and turn a lot."

There was something in what she said. The road did wind a good deal, as it followed the bends of the river, and there were frequent hills and blind turns. The pavement, after the winter frosts, was in pretty bad shape — full of potholes and frost-bumps which were apt to throw you into the ditch if you weren't careful.

I'd been doing close to fifty-five since getting past the city limits, but I slowed down in response to my wife's warning and began to take in the scenery again. The road on this side of the river was on a high level, and you got a grand view right across the valley to the rolling wooded hills on the horizon. The land across the river was dotted with white and yellow farmhouses and their huddled grey barns; here and there you could see farmers on tractors or behind teams of horses rhythmically moving back and forth across the fields as they did the spring seeding.

But I was feeling too gay to drive slowly for long. The speedometer crept up to forty-five, fifty, fifty-five, and was just crowding sixty when we hit the worst pothole yet. I thought for a moment that I'd lost control of the car; we were within an ace of hitting the near ditch; but I managed to cling to the steering wheel and swing it hard round to the left. As I did so, I suddenly became aware of a kid on a bicycle on that side. I missed him all right, but it was a close shave that left me sweating all over.

"Golly, Daddy," said Jimmy, "that was a close one!"

"I told you to be careful," said Edith. "You almost spoiled the first picnic right there!"

Well, I settled down after that and coasted along at about thirty-five. After about half an hour of steady driving we began to look out for a place to picnic. We saw several possibilities, but when we stopped to examine them there was always something missing. Finally we saw just the right spot. There was a high point of land jutting into the river; on this point were two quite large buildings, one white and new looking, the other old and grey; and on this side of them there was a nice open space which would be just right for a game of ball, and a patch of pebbly beach which would be ideal for the fire and the kids' boats.

I turned in the driveway beside the buildings and parked close to the water.

The kids pulled off their socks and shoes and were paddling in the water and pulling their boats around in no time. After I'd gathered driftwood for the fire I sat down on the rug beside Edith and watched the kids playing.

We looked out across the water, which was flowing slowly and silently southward, and on me at least it had its usual soothing effect. I forgot all about the near-crash with the car and settled down into one of those rare moods in which body and mind and the whole world seem to be functioning in perfect harmony. The breeze had increased slightly, and now blew in occasional gusts which turned up white patches of foam like the flash of birds' wings. But the gusts were warm and fragrant with spring, and did not disturb but rather emphasized the peaceful, rhythmic beauty of the day.

"I wonder what those buildings behind us are?" asked Edith.

I looked back at them. The nearer one, white and new, might have been one of the new Regional High Schools which were springing up all over the province, though if so it was unusually small. But why the old grey building? It was too large for a teacher's or janitor's house, and it didn't look like an old school, with its many small windows. It looked more like an old farmhouse, but there were no barns or outbuildings to go with it.

"I don't know," I said. "They might be schools, but it hardly seems likely."

"That's probably it," said Edith. "That would explain why they're so quiet. Saturday, school's out and the teacher's in town shopping."

I shrugged my shoulders and turned again to the playing kids, the flowing river, and the rolling hills beyond. But my mood had been broken. I couldn't get those buildings off my mind. I kept gnawing away, trying to figure them out. Maybe the white one was a community hall or centre of some kind — but again, why the old grey building so close by?

"Shucks," I said. "It's beyond me! Let's eat!"

I lit the fire and put the kettle on while Edith got the hamburg and the rolls and the other food out of the hamper. As usual, the food tasted twice as good outdoors, and in the joy of eating and watching the kids eat far more than the normal amount I forgot all about the puzzling buildings.

After we had cleared up, I suggested a game of ball before starting for home.

Jimmy took charge as usual on such occasions. "O.K., dad. I'll pitch. Mummy, you're catcher. Susan, out in the field. Daddy, you're at bat. And don't hit it too far now."

We took our places. Jimmy wound up in real big league fashion, but the pitch was too high for me to reach even with the bat above my head. Edith recovered the ball from the edge of the water and Jimmy wound up again. This time the ball rolled along the ground and went through the catcher's legs — much to the delight of the pitcher and outfielder. The third pitch, however, was just right, and I caught the ball squarely. It sailed into the air, landed on the grass near the grey building, and rolled right to the wall.

Susan and Jimmy both ran after it, but apparently neither of them had seen just where it went and they were searching around helplessly. I went over to pick it up for them.

"There it is," I said, pointing it out by the wall. The kids made a dive for it.

At that moment I became aware of a movement in the window above them, and noticed for the first time that the window was crossed by iron bars. Then the window was pushed up, and a man's face appeared whitely against the bars.

"Hello!" he said.

"How do you do?" I stammered foolishly, while the kids stared up at him with wide curious eyes.

"Your kids?" he said.

I nodded.

"Like a stick of gum?" He fumbled with a package in his hands.

"Sure!" came the duet, and hands reached eagerly up towards the bars.

He looked at me. "Is it O.K.?"

I nodded again, though I knew Edith would disapprove. She hated them to have gum, for it always ended up in their hair or on their clothes.

He held two sticks of gum out through the bars, and I handed them down to the kids. I touched his fingers as I took the gum, and they were cold and clammy. I couldn't help a slight shudder of revulsion, but the kids hastily unwrapped the gum and started chewing it with obvious satisfaction.

"A nice pair of kids," he said.

I could sense Edith's impatience far behind me on the beach, but the man obviously wanted to talk. I couldn't think of anything to say and looked nervously around for a warden or some other official, but apart from the one window there was no sign of life anywhere.

I half turned towards Edith and the river. "You get a lovely view from here," I said awkwardly.

"Yes," he said. "But it gets tiresome after a while." A slight smile for the first time shifted the corners of his mouth.

"Been here long?" I said. Maybe he was the warden himself. Maybe he had just been cleaning up the cell or something.

"Since last November," he said. "Waiting for trial. Just missed one session of the court, so I have to wait for the next. Should be along any day now."

Well, that settled one problem. He was no warden. There was another question I very much wanted to ask, but conscious of the eagerly listening children I repressed it in favour of a third.

"What's that classy white building in front?"

"That's the Court House. That's where the trial will be."

"John, what are you doing?" It was Edith, calling from the beach. She was starting towards us. I should have to go. I blurted out the real question in spite of the children.

"What are you in for?"

"I killed a man."

The children moved still closer to the window — or was it that I involuntarily had stepped back?

"Killed?" I said. "How?"

Thank heaven Edith wasn't close enough yet to hear me! What a question to ask in front of the children!

"Ran him down with a truck." He leaned forward confidentially until his forehead touched the bars. "I had the boss's truck out for the evening, see? He didn't know, and I wasn't supposed to drive it — but you know how it is. There was this dame I kindov liked lived down the road here a ways, and I drove down to see her with a few quarts of beer. We had a nice time, a few drinks — not many, but enough to make us feel good. Around eleven, I started home, and found the lights on the truck wouldn't work. Up the road here a piece, I felt a bit of a bump. I was going kindov fast, and didn't pay much attention. I thought likely it had been a dog or something, maybe even a mailbox. Anyway I didn't stop. Next morning the police were around before I was up. They'd picked this old guy up by the side of the road. There was blood and hair on the rear-vision mirror of the truck, so what could I say?"

He stared at me from his tired grey eyes as if he hoped I could provide an answer. I could only stare back, shifting uneasily from foot to foot. I knew Edith must be near, and I was anxious to be gone.

"The trial will be on whithin a week or two," he went on, as if anxious not to lose me. "You watch for it in the papers. They'll find me guilty, all right, and then it'll be Colchester for a stretch."

He would have gone on, but I could hear Edith's footsteps just behind me, so I broke away from him. "Best of luck," I said lamely. "And I'll sure watch for it in the papers!"

"That's right," he called after us. "You watch for it. And be good kids, now, you two."

The kids were all for lingering, but I pulled them along beside me. I could feel the pull of his eyes on my back, too.

I tried to keep it from Edith, but of course she got the whole story out of me. She was furious. "Fancy standing there all this time talking to a man like that! The children, too. Why, he's nothing but a common murderer!"

"Manslaughter..." I protested, but she wouldn't listen. She made the kids spit out the gum at once.

I had been so engrossed in the man and his story that I hadn't noticed the way the weather was changing. The breeze had quickened to a wind that whipped the water till it threw out a pus-like foam, and the smoke-like clouds had thickened and darkened so that they now completely blocked out the sun.

As we drove out on to the highway, spatters of rain began to beat on the windshield. Soon it was falling heavily. Edith sat glumly beside me. I knew she was disgusted with me, but that would soon wear off. It wasn't that that was bothering me, nor even the rain.

I drove slowly and carefully. How easy it would be! In the dark, perhaps a wet night like this, driving an old truck without lights and probably with poor brakes, thinking of the woman and careless from the beer. And then the sudden bump. There would be that long, long moment while he wondered "What was that? I hit something. A dog? A skunk? Maybe it was..." But by that time he would be a quarter of a mile up the road, nowhere to turn around, the rain and the darkness behind and a warm bed waiting at home, and naturally, what with the beer and all, you hoped for the best and you — or he, who was it driving the truck now, you or he? — didn't stop though deep down you knew you should have, that you would deserve everything that was coming to you if it came.

I looked across at Edith. Was she still disgusted, or was she, too, now that her irritation had worn off, thinking about the man in the cell, and the nightmare of the trial after all these months of solitary fretting, and the prospect of years in Colchester, staring out across the marshes to the sea?

In the back seat the children were laughing and singing.

"Why don't you sing, Dad? Boy, didn't we have fun today? Wait till I tell the kids at school!"

"Daddy," said Susan. "You know what I think? I think that was the best picnic yet!"

She whispered in my ear and secretly showed me something clasped in her hand. It was the green wrapper from the stick of gum.

The Boat

The boy Gerald pushed back his plate across the brown oilcloth, nearly upsetting his empty milk glass.

His aunt glared at him with cold grey eyes. "Watch yourself!" she said in her thin, edgy voice.

His uncle looked up from his dish at the end of the table. "What's he up to now?"

"Nearly broke another glass. We'll soon have none left."

His uncle grunted and went on eating his rice pudding in large spoonfuls.

The boy caught the eye of the hired man across the table, and a slight smile passed between them. The aunt noticed the smile and looked at them suspiciously, but the boy spoke to the man in spite of her.

"Don't forget what you promised to do today," said the boy.

"I haven't forgotten. We'll go as soon as I'm finished."

The aunt, quick and sharp as a pecking bird, picked it up. "What's that? What are you going to do?"

The hired man lifted his round, ruddy face and answered her. "Make a boat," he said, slowly. "I promised I'd make him a boat today. Then we'll sail her in the creek."

The woman was silenced for a moment by the man's frankness, but the uncle spoke up. "A boat?" he said. "What are you making boats for? Has he been pestering you? I should think you'd have to do without making boats."

"It's no trouble," said the man. "I like making boats."

"Huh! More fool you then, that's all I can say. Rest while you can, I say. We get little enough of it." He pushed his chair back noisily and went off into the parlour with his weekly farm magazine.

"Boats!" muttered his aunt disdainfully, as she began to gather up the dishes before the hired man was quite finished. "I wonder what next? And on the Lord's Day, too."

The hired man and the boy went out of the kitchen together, into the warm glow of the summer sunshine. They walked across the strip of lawn to the barnyard and past the heavily fragrant stump of last year's straw-stack. Some grey hens lay sunning themselves in the straw; others were vigorously dusting themselves in pockets of sand beside it. The boy had to take quick steps to keep up with the slow steady stride of the man's long legs.

They came to the machine-shed, and the man pulled back the heavy sliding door. Inside it was cool and dark and the air smelt of oil and old leather and rusty iron. On the packed earth floor, between drill and mower and other out-of-season implements, were tins of nails, boxes of nuts and scraps of broken harness, scattered pieces of wood left from various repair jobs.

Tom began to rummage among the debris, searching for a bit of wood suitable for the boat-making. Gerald sat on an upturned empty nail-keg, watching. They did not speak. They had had enough of sharp, pecking chatter from the woman in the house.

Tom found a rectangular piece of wood about a foot long, and held it up for Gerald to see. Then he began to carve it with his big horn-handled clasp-knife. Magically the boat took shape, moulded patiently to form under Tom's skillful fingers. He worked at it until he had shaped a tapering keel, a pointed bow, and a gently rounded stern. Then he sandpapered the hull all over, until it was silky smooth. Last of all he made three holes in the middle of the deck and cut three thin masts to fit them. He regarded the finished boat carefully and then handed it to the boy.

"Isn't she a beauty?" said Gerald. "What shall we call her?"

"You name her," said Tom. "You're better with words than I am."

"How about the *Good Hope*? That sounds like a three-master to me!"

"Good enough," said Tom. "The *Good Hope* she is."

They went out again into the sunshine, walking down the lane towards the back of the farm. The boy clutched the boat in his hands, feeling its rounded smoothness beneath his fingers. They passed lines of stooks stretched across the stubble fields, the grey-green surfaces of cleared hay-fields, the tall dark green stalks of the growing corn. In the full heat of the August afternoon, the landscape lay tranquil and silent.

They came then to the back pasture, where the black and white cows were chewing their cuds in the shade of the hickory trees. "Better get a stick," said Tom. "We'll need one to steer her along the creek."

They each selected a long stick, and then went on to the bank of the narrow winding stream which cut diagonally across the pasture.

"The bridge'll be the best place to launch her," said Tom.

They walked along the bank until they came to the home-made plank bridge, slung across the creek so that the cows might cross from this section of the pasture to the other.

Gerald held out the boat. "You launch her," he said.

"No, you do it! Just lean over the water and give her a little push."

The boy knelt on the planks, holding the boat as if it were made of thin glass, then leaned over and let it slide into the water. Its bow dipped for a moment; then it began to glide smoothly forward in the current.

The man and the boy, one on each side of the creek, followed the course of the boat as it nosed its way downstream towards the river. Most of the time it ran freely, but occasionally it was caught by a water-weed. When this happened, the sticks came into play, and the boat was quickly dislodged and started onward again. Tom walked soberly on his side, but the boy danced along his bank, waving his stick in the air, cheering the *Good Hope* on. He imagined the boat now as a Spanish galleon, its crew lusting for gold and spices; now as the craft of Drake, seeking honour and wealth for the Virgin Queen; now as a pirate ship seen hull-down, laden with treasure, and with Long John Silver numbered amongst its crew.

The creek broadened and ran more swiftly as it neared the broad river which marked the rear boundary of his uncle's farm.

The boat began to move more rapidly, racing in the swift current. The boy's excitement grew, and he cheered the vessel on more loudly than ever. But suddenly, before they were aware of the danger, the boat was swept out into the current of the river itself. Swiftly it was drawn farther and farther from shore, beyond the reach of their outstretched sticks.

"Oh, Tom," the boy cried, "we've lost her."

"Don't worry," said Tom. "I'll fetch her back." He had already pulled off his shoes and socks, and was rolling up his Sunday trousers above his knees. In less than a minute he had begun to wade out into the river.

The boy watched carefully as the man waded still farther out into the swift brown water. The water was up to his knees already, and he was not halfway to the *Good Hope*. In the boy's eyes now the proud three-master was only a tiny, bobbing, brown speck. But Tom kept wading after it, yet farther out into the current, until the water was well up above his rolled trousers. It was around his waist now, and still the boat was out of reach. It seemed to the boy that at any moment Tom must lose his footing in the strong current.

"Come back, Tom!" he called. "Come back! Let the boat go!"

He was startled by the sound of his own voice in the tense silence of the afternoon, but if Tom heard the shout he paid no attention. Man and boat now were both beyond the boy's reach, and he stood helpless on the bank, his fists clenched and his face set.

Tom waded steadily on, in water which now almost reached his armpits. At last he grasped the boat and, turning, held it up triumphantly for Gerald to see.

But, as he held it aloft, he suddenly lurched forward, as if his foot had struck a submerged rock. For one long horrible moment it seemed that he must be swept away and be carried under the water which, even in the glare of the hot summer sun, looked cold and dark and evil.

Then somehow the man recovered his balance and began to edge his way towards the shore, clutching the precious boat carefully against his chest.

Once he was safe again, Tom dried his clothes in the sunshine. "Don't say anything to your aunt about this," he said.

"Of course not," said the boy. "But weren't you scared, Tom?"

"Nothing to be scared of in a bit of water, is there?"

They took the boat up to the bridge again, and launched her as before. This time, however, they were more cautious, and took her out of the creek before she could reach the treacherous river.

The summer holidays had come to an end, and now the first term of a new school year was more than half over. Already Gerald was looking forward to the Christmas holidays, and hoping that Tom would be better by then and able to make him the sleigh he had promised.

For the hired man was very ill. His aunt wouldn't often let Gerald in to see him, but when he did get into Tom's room he was scared by the man's flushed cheeks and strangely bright eyes. His face had lost its round fullness, and was thin and drawn.

One evening in late November, an unseasonably mild day when the grey rain had washed the light covering of snow from the fields and had left them brown and bare, the boy was sitting at the supper table with his aunt and uncle. His aunt had just come down with a tray from Tom's room.

"A fine thing this is," she said sharply. "Me waiting hand and foot on a hired man every day. It's nearly two weeks now he's been stuck in bed. I've enough to do around here without playing the nurse all the time."

"How does he seem?" asked the uncle.

"Looks about the same to me. Still running a high fever, and he eats hardly enough to keep a sparrow alive."

"Doctor in today?"

"Yes. He didn't say much. More pills, and keep giving him lots of liquids till the fever goes down."

"Did he say anything about the hospital?"

"He said it would be better not to move him the way he is now, but he may have to if he's not improved in a day or two. I don't like the look of him, I can tell you. His eyes are so bright they fair frighten me."

The conversation went on, but the boy took no part in it. He felt as lost and helpless as he had felt that day on the bank of the river.

Suddenly the door from upstairs opened, and the boy caught a quick terrifying glimpse of the hired man, his eyes wild, his nightshirt dangling grotesquely about his knees. Before Gerald could move or even speak, the hired man had run across the kitchen and had disappeared through the back door into the wet darkness.

All sense of living had fled from the boy, and he heard his aunt and uncle as if from a great distance.

"What?" said his aunt, in a curiously muffled voice. She looked helplessly towards her husband.

His uncle had jumped from his chair. "Delirious," he said. "It's the fever." His wife ran towards him, but he pushed her aside and followed the hired man into the night.

The boy had come to himself again. "I must go, too," he said, starting for the door.

"Oh, no, you don't," said his aunt, seizing his arm and holding him with all her strength. "It's no place for a nine-year-old boy."

He stood staring at her furiously, his will hard set against hers. She let go of him, and then, in a soft, tired voice quite unlike her usual sharp tone, she said: "I know you want to help, but you'll only hinder. Your uncle will find him if he's to be found. Do your homework and see how your uncle makes out."

Mechanically he cleared a place for his books and tried to concentrate on his homework. His aunt was at the sink doing the dishes.

His uncle returned at last, alone, his soaked shirt plastered against his arms and back, the rain-water streaming from his black hair. "Not a trace of him," he said wearily. "I was too late to see which way he went, and it's pitch black out there. I've called all through the barns and about the garden, but there was no answer. Light a lantern for me, Esther."

"Are you going out again?"

"Yes. We can't leave him out on a night like this. I'll call some of the neighbours, too. Between us we might find him."

The boy watched and listened as his aunt lit the lantern and his uncle made the telephone calls. When he took the lantern and started for the door again, the boy asked, "May I come with you?"

"No, lad, it's no job for you. Get on with your homework!"

He turned again to his books, but they meant nothing to him tonight. He kept straining his ears for a sound from outdoors, but heard nothing.

At ten o'clock, when there was still no sign of his uncle, his aunt sent him up to bed. He fled swiftly up the narrow stairs and undressed with quick, fumbling fingers. The dim light of the coal-oil lamp left shadowy, fear-filled corners in his small room. And then, propped against the small mirror of his pine dresser, he noticed the boat. He took it in his hands, blew out the lamp, and dived into the damp bed. He pulled the covers over his head, and hugged the smooth boat tightly to his chest.

They did not find Tom that night, nor the next day, Saturday. The rain had washed away his footprints: it was impossible to tell which way he had gone.

The men of the neighbourhood had split into two groups, one to search the fields and the patches of bushland, while the other, led by the boy's uncle, dragged the river.

His uncle forbade Gerald to join either group and warned him especially to stay away from the river. All day Saturday he wandered about the fields alone, clutching the boat.

Another night passed; Sunday dawned dull and cold. A slow, unceasing wind mourned around the house, and sent the branches of the elms into a melancholy dance. Again the boy slowly circled the fields, but he knew it was no use looking there. In spite of his uncle's warning he drew closer and closer to the river.

He came to the pasture and to the creek where he and Tom had sailed the boat. In the grey light of the November afternoon he stood on the plank bridge where they had launched her, and looked towards the river. He could see his uncle and the three neighbours, dragging the dark water from an old rowboat.

Suddenly he heard a shout from the boat, and saw the seated men spring to their feet. They were hauling something from the water.

They began to row toward the shore, and he ran down beside the bank of the creek to meet them. He stood on the shore of the river and waited, as he had waited when Tom waded after the boat. The men did not notice him, so intent were they on the object in the bottom of their boat.

The rowboat scraped to a halt, and the men began to lift out the drowned body of the hired man. The striped nightshirt still clung to the cold limbs.

Again the boy had that timeless sensation of paralyzed helplessness. It was his uncle who broke the spell. As if he had realized for the first time that Gerald was there, he suddenly shouted, "What are you doing here? Didn't I tell you to stay away from the river? Get back to the house and stay there!"

The boy turned and ran stumblingly along the bank of the creek. He did not stop until he came to the bridge. There he paused and looked back at the small group of men, still bending about the body of the hired man.

When he saw that he held in his hand the boat which the hired man had fashioned for him, he fingered a little the smooth curves of her hull and felt her three tiny graceful masts. Then he lifted his arm and threw the *Good Hope* with all his strength down the stream towards the dark river.

That Day in the Bush

He awoke with the feeling that this day was to be somehow special. He found it hard to account for the feeling, however. It was New Year's Eve, but that was not an occasion of which they took much notice on the farm. There would be no party that night, and he and his parents would probably go to bed as usual well before midnight. Still, the feeling persisted.

He dressed quickly in his overalls, workshirt and sweater, and went downstairs. His father had already lit the kitchen stove and the boy sat close to it as he put on his shoes. Then, slipping on his cap and mackinaw coat, he went out to the barn.

The barn was warm and moist with the breath of horses and cattle, and full of a predominantly pleasant odour made up of the mingled scents of hay, ensilage, and straw.

"What's the programme for today, Dad?" he asked his father, as he prepared his first cow for milking.

"Cut a few trees back in the bush, I guess."

"Good!" he said, and meant it. He started to whistle as he sat down beside the cow and began rhythmically to milk her. A day in the bush was what he most enjoyed in the Christmas holiday from high school. Perhaps that was why he had had the special feeling of elation.

After breakfast he and his father collected the cross-cut saw and two axes in the machine shed and headed for the bush. It was a perfect morning for cutting wood. The air was crisp and clear, there was no wind, and the temperature was well above zero. The snow was fresh but not deep enough to be a nuisance: about two inches had fallen in the night and made a loose brilliant covering over the three or four inches of more closely-packed old snow beneath.

The youth and the man trudged silently down the lane, each deep in his own thoughts. It seemed to the boy that the farm had never looked so beautiful. The branches of the hickory, maple, and elm trees beside the lane and along the fences in the fields were powdered with the light snow. The dark grey barns of the next farm stood out in vivid outline against the white background of the surrounding fields. Here and there were clumps of bush, a dull blue-grey against the brighter and lighter blue of the sky.

There was a trance-like quality in the whole scene. They alone moved; they alone made a sound as their boots crunched softly in the snow. The fence-posts, like sentinels, kept watch over the silent fields.

They came to the end of the lane and began to walk over the little hills and hollows of the bush.

"Where do we start, Dad?"

"Let's take out this ash first. It's beginning to rot — look at those branches near the top."

His father chopped a wedge out of one side of the tree, and then they picked up the cross-cut saw and began to pull it back and forth against the other side. Pull, let slide, pull, let slide, pull, let slide — the slow rhythm of the saw seemed to blend with and even to enhance the dream-like atmosphere of the day. The light yellow sawdust dribbled out of the cut as he pulled his saw back, dribbled out in firm serrated fragments which gradually formed a dark yellow stain as they mingled with the snow. The fresh sweet scent of the sawdust was pungent in his nostrils.

His feet melted the snow beneath them, and he began to slip a bit. He shifted his feet to get a firmer stance. Pull, let slide, pull, let slide, pull, let slide. They kept sawing steadily until they were halfway through the trunk.

"All right, take a rest," said his Dad.

The boy let go of the handle and straightened his back. All around them the trees stood draped in snow. He looked back towards the barns and house. Nothing moved except the thin ribbon of smoke which rose straight upward from the house chimney. From the railway track a mile away came the low wail of a passing freight, the slow faint thunder of its turning wheels: the sounds spread in slow circles over the fields, then as gradually withdrew, narrowed again to silence.

"Ready, boy?"

"Sure."

They bent again to the saw. Pull, let slide, pull, let slide. The sawdust edged its way from the cut, fell to the snow, and mingled. Then there was a faint cracking sound, and the cut began to widen almost imperceptibly. He let go of the handle, his father pulled out the saw, and they both stepped backward at right angles to the path of the falling tree.

Slowly, gracefully, lithely the tree tilted forward. Then suddenly it seemed to gather momentum, fell rapidly with a quick swoosh, a sharp cracking of branches, and a crashing sound that was almost deafening after the long silence. It bounced slightly as it hit the ground, then lay immobile.

"May as well cut it up while we're at it," his father said. They took their axes and trimmed off the smaller limbs, then began to saw up the larger branches and the trunk into four-foot lenghts for hauling.

"Now what?" the boy asked, as the last piece of trunk was sawn.

"I don't know. There's that birch over by the fence. It's going to be tricky, but this might be the best day to try it."

"What's tricky about it?"

"Well, it leans a bit towards the fence, and it's so close that if it falls that way it will smash the fence to bits. But it's not a big tree, and it's not leaning badly, and on a day like this, with no wind to bother us, we should be able to shove it over."

"I'm game."

"O.K. Let's go."

They carried the axes and saw across to the tree by the fence.

His father circled the tree, sizing it up.

"Maybe we'd better leave it," he said. "We might get a day when the wind's from the west and would help us."

"It doesn't look much of a problem to me," said the boy. And it didn't. It was little more than twenty feet high, and no more than eight inches in diameter at its base. It had few branches, and they were bunched near the top. Its lean backwards towards the fence was almost imperceptible.

His father continued to consider the problem, nevertheless. He paced off the distance to the fence, put his hands against the trunk as if to decide how easily it would push, looked vaguely around at the other trees as if wondering which of them to cut if he passed this one up.

The boy, a little impatient at the delay, looked around the fields. Everything was still and silent as ever: the snowdraped trees, the grey barns, the thin straight ribbon of smoke from the house. He drank in the fresh cool air, flexed his arms and shoulders, felt flow through him a wave of well-being. What a day! he thought to himself. No wonder it had seemed somehow special.

"What do you think, boy?" Want to chance it?"

"Sure. What have we to lose? Even if it does fall the wrong way we shall only have broken a few feet of fence."

"All right. I'll notch her low down and hope for the best."

His father took the axe and notched the tree near the ground on the far side from the fence. Then they bent together to the handles of the saw, began again their rhythmic motion. Pull and let slide, pull and let slide, pull and let slide. The sawdust began to dribble out of the cut, but this time it took the form not of firm serrated fragments but of a fine dust, and instead of being light yellow this dust was reddish brown. Its stain on the snow was almost the colour of blood; its odour was musty and decayed.

They stopped sawing before they were half way through the trunk. "Watch her, boy," his father said. "She's rotten, and she might fall any minute. Be ready to step back smartly when she starts to go." Then they both looked up at the tree as if they hoped to read in its branches what it would finally do. As they stared, a small gust of wind moved the branches slightly, and there fell into their upturned faces tiny fragments of lacy snow.

They shifted their feet to get a firmer stance, then bent again to the handles of the saw. Once more they began to pull the saw back and forth through the cut, but no longer with the same quick steady motion. Now they pulled slowly, jerkily, warily. The boy felt his nerves and muscles grow tense and taut.

For a surprising length of time the tree stood and gave no sign of falling. In the intervals of their sawing, the boy swept the landscape with his gaze, seeking to regain that sense of magic which had been drowned in his rising fear. But the white land, the grey barns, and the blue sky seemed now only blank, dull, and lonely. The thin ribbon of smoke from the house wavered from time to time in the intermittent wind.

Suddenly there was a stronger gust of wind, a great rush of air from the east. Sickeningly, terrifyingly, the boy knew that the tree was falling towards him. He didn't think to step aside out of the tree's path, instead, in blind panic, he ran in the line of its fall. Vaguely he heard a shout of warning, but he was past responding to it. He sensed the trunk descending on him, knew too late that he had moved the wrong way. Desperately he tried to fling himself out of its path, but in the split second before darkness drowned him had time only to realize that this was the special gift the treacherous day had brought him.

When She Comes Over

He had waited for her all Fall and Winter, and now in a month she would be coming over. It was time he was looking for a flat. It would be so good to get away from the dreary set of rooms at the boarding-house of the Misses York, and into a home of their own. All alone with Elizabeth! What a life that would be!

So on a bright May afternoon he skipped his usual mission to the University Library and visited a real estate agent off Market Square. Armed with a short list of vacant, unfurnished flats, he left the agent's office and began the exciting hunt. From one address to another he pedalled, pretending to a series of landlords and caretakers that he was an old hand at this game, and knew all about stoves and water heaters and rooms with a view.

None of the first six flats quite suited him. 88 Wordsworth Walk — perhaps this would be lucky seven! It was a large semi-detached grey brick house, set back in a small garden. A note on the agent's list said that the key to the vacant upstairs flat was to be obtained from the occupant of the downstairs flat, Mrs. Monahan.

He opened the cast-iron gate and knocked at the basement door, a bright green door with a shiny brass knocker. The door opened, and a young woman with auburn hair and breasts that pouted against her yellow sweater popped out like a cuckoo from a clock.

He jumped back in surprise, then stammered, "Are you Mrs. Monahan?"

"Yes," she smiled warmly. "Can I help you?" She said this as if she really meant it, not with the feigned, slightly servile politeness of most of the caretakers.

"I'm to look at the upstairs flat. Ritchies gave me the address. Their list says you have the key." He held the list out for her inspection.

"Of course," she said, "It'll be a pleasure!" There was a lilt of the Irish in her tongue. "Come in a moment while I find the key."

He stepped into the hall and admired its glossy linoleum floor and clean grey walls while he waited for Mrs. Monahan to return.

"Here you are," she said, holding out the key in long slender fingers.

His own hand, for some reason, shook slightly as he took the key from her. "I'll bring it right back," he promised, avoiding her eyes.

"Oh, don't hurry. I'll be in all afternoon. Have a good look around upstairs. And I hope you'll like it!"

Well, Mrs. Monahan would sure make a friendly neighbour for Elizabeth when she came over. He could imagine the two of them having coffee together in the mornings, and tea in the afternoons.

He knew at once, when he entered the upstairs flat, that it was just the place he had been looking for. There was a large living room with a fireplace and a big bay window that gave a fine view of Cambridge and its colleges, a small but surprisingly well equipped kitchen, a bathroom with a gas water heater, and up on the third floor a huge bedroom with all sorts of odd nooks and crannies occasioned by the angles of the roof.

He poked around for half an hour or so imagining what it would be like to sit with Elizabeth on a chesterfield beside the fireplace, to eat with her in the tiny kitchen, to lie with her upstairs in the quaint old bedroom...

When he took the key back to Mrs. Monahan, she said, "Oh, thanks. Did you like the flat?"

"It's lovely," he said. "Just what I was looking for!"

"And you're going to take it?"

"Yes, I just hope Elizabeth likes it when she comes over!"

"Elizabeth? Your wife?"

He blushed. "Not yet. My fiancée."

"Oh, do tell me about her! Come in and tell me. I've just put the kettle on. We can have some tea in a minute."

He hesitated. "I should get back to the agent's. I've a lot of work I should be doing — I'm a research student, and I really should be at work in the library."

"Oh, the work will wait for a while, I'm sure. Come on in and chat a bit."

He went in and sat on a gaily covered chesterfield in her snug living-room, while she bustled about in the kitchen. Now this was really homey! What a change from the cabbage smells and the faded brocade of the establishment of the eccentric Misses York!

She came in bearing a silver tea service, and set it down on a small table near him. While she poured the tea, she said, "Now tell me about Elizabeth! Is she coming over from the States?"

"No, from Canada." It was not like him to be so reticent, but he was beginning to be a bit suspicious of this woman. She was, as the manager in the Coop had said of another lately, "a bit too sweet to be wholesome." To talk of Elizabeth to her seemed almost indecent, like a profanation.

"I'll bet she's as pretty as a picture."

"She's nice-looking, all right."

"And when does she get here?"

"In less than a month now. On the tenth of June. She has to finish her exams."

"So she's a student too. How nice for you! You'll be a lovely couple. I'm sure I shall love her. What is she like?"

Gradually she drew him out, gradually he lost his distrust of her — though not, altogether, his wariness. It was the first time in eight months that he had talked to a young woman: his landladies were both over sixty, and even the women who waited on him in the shops were usually twice his age. He wondered how much older than his own twenty-two Mrs. Monahan was. She might be twenty-four, or at most twenty-six. But he remained wary of her, wary of his own instinctive pleasure in the soft curve of her pouting breasts and in the brightness of her eyes. What was the expression in those eyes? Friendly interest? Natural good spirits? Or something more personal, more intimate than this — a hint of deliberate seductiveness, perhaps? Nonsense, he told himself — but be wary nevertheless. It would not do to be unfaithful to Elizabeth now, after eight months of celibacy — now, just as she was coming over.

After an hour in her admittedly pleasant company, he returned to the agent's office to sign the lease.

It had been nice talking to Mrs. Monahan, and she was probably just a warmhearted Irish girl who loved her husband and had nothing but a perfectly innocent friendly interest in him. Still, it would be wise to try avoiding her in future. When Elizabeth came over, there would be plenty of time for them to get to know their neighbours. Meanwhile, he would keep to himself. There was dynamite in that smile, in those slowly-swinging, proudly-pouting breasts...

* * *

But to stay away from Mrs. Monahan was more easily planned than performed. Now that the apartment was his, he found himself going almost every day to visit it, to sit on the ledge in the bay window reading, and dream of how it would be when Elizabeth came over. And although he now had his own key and tried to slip in and out unnoticed, Nora — as she insisted he call her — almost always seemed to see him. She would tap on her window, or come out into the little front garden, and ask him if he had heard from Elizabeth and how his work at the library was going and whether there was anything she could do to help him get the flat ready; and if it was in the morning she would ask him for a cup of coffee, and if in the afternoon to share a cup of tea with her.

Within a week or two they had become fast friends. She told him that they should become friends because they were both lonely. He was waiting for his fiancée to come over from Canada, and she was home alone a great deal because her husband was a commercial traveller and out of town almost every weekday. He found out that she was twenty-five and had been married three years — what a coincidence that they were both to marry at twenty-two! And she came from Belfast and had intended to become an interior decorator but she'd met Jim Monahan while on a visit to an aunt's in Liverpool and he'd swept her off her feet (such a passionate fellow he was and not to be denied) and she'd married him within a month and here she was in Cambridge all alone all week just living for the weekends until Ben came along and it was so nice to have someone to talk to and wouldn't it be nice when Elizabeth came over because when Ben was away studying in the library Nora and Elizabeth would be able to go shopping together and have their afternoon tea. And Ben in his turn told her how he'd got his degree from Queen's last year and Elizabeth was finishing her senior year now and as soon as her exams were over (she wasn't even going to wait for the graduation exercises because eight months was long enough to wait and actually having the diploma handed to you personally didn't make any difference) she was coming over and in fact she'd be sailing next Saturday just six days from now and in another six she'd be here and yes it would be so much fun for Elizabeth to have Nora to show her the ropes and help her to get on to pounds and pence and lifts and left-hand drivers.

And Ben told Nora (he sitting on the easy chair covered in the same pretty figured slip-cover as the chesterfield and she leaning back on the latter as if they'd known each other for years as indeed they now felt) about his problem of the furniture. Furnished apartments were just too expensive, and yet the second-hand furniture he'd hoped to buy seemed so cheap and ugly and broken down looking and he hated to think of Elizabeth seeing *that* when she came over.

So Nora suggested that she go with him — after all, she had begun to study interior decorating and she did have pretty good taste if she said it herself — and they'd see what *she* could find. And so most of the afternoons of the next week they spent going from shop to shop and Nora found this sweet little occasional chair here and that awfully attractive little rug there and a lamp that would be just right for the bay window and a whole lot of things that would give Elizabeth such a lovely surprise when she came over.

By the Friday afternoon the last of the furniture had been delivered and when Ben came up to look the place over Nora tapped at the window and came out and said she thought they really ought to celebrate having finished the job and that if Ben would put the first fire on in the fireplace she'd come up in a few minutes with a real surprise. And he put the fire on and she came up with a shaker of martinis and two glasses on a tray and she said Jim would be home tomorrow and Elizabeth would be sailing and so today was in a sense *their* day and they'd worked so hard together they deserved a little treat. And Ben drew the dear little chesterfield she'd chosen up before the fire and they sat and watched the logs blazing and drank a martini and then another and another until the bottle was empty and they both felt as if they had known each other for years and years and at last Nora suggested they go up and see how the bedroom was going to look when she came over and they giggled and went upstairs and Nora flounced on the bed and said come on and try it and he did and he had to admit it felt good and that she had good taste in beds and he'd bet Elizabeth would say the same when she came over...

On the Roman Road

When the message came, in the middle of Saturday morning in April, Henry could at first feel nothing — there was only a terrible kind of blankness, as if all the rhythms of life had stopped. The rest of the day loomed ahead dully, a desert stretch of time that must somehow be traversed.

And then he thought of the Roman road. Bill, his fifteen year old son, had been saying for weeks that the family must go out there — the boy had discovered it on a Scout hike, had found the abandoned road exciting and wanted the family to share his excitement. Henry could feel no strong interest in it today, but it would be something to do, it would be better than pacing back and forth in the house like this.

As soon as they had had lunch they piled into the car and headed for the Gog Magog hills, that ridge on the outskirts of Cambridge which is so peculiar a feature in the otherwise flat landscape of the Fen country.

Following Bill's directions, Henry parked the big Canadian station wagon on a suburban side street, and the family followed Bill to the end of the street and on to a narrow pathway bordered by high bushes — all that was left at this point of the old Roman road. It was apparent that very few people came this way any more, for the path was barely detectable and in many places was almost blocked by overhanging branches.

The April day was muggily warm, but the usual Cambridge haze covered the sun, and the surrounding fields, glimpsed from time to time through breaks in the bushes, still had that faint, washed-out colouring which marks the landscape of early spring.

Bill and the three younger children, Helen, John and Jane, ran on ahead, sometimes darting off the path into the bushes, doubling back, playing hide and seek, occasionally squealing with surprise or pleasure. Henry felt like telling them to be quiet — after all, hadn't he told them about the message, couldn't they realize how he was feeling? — but he felt so listless that he couldn't be bothered even to reproach them. Elizabeth, his wife, walked quietly in front of him — the pathway was too narrow to walk two abreast — speaking only when the children asked her a direct question and then saying as little as possible. Henry, even in his present lethargy, felt a twinge of love and appreciation of her tact — he could sense that she knew his mood, that she realized it was no time for idle chatter.

Henry at first took in almost nothing of his surroundings. He had put the message in the pocket of his shirt and it seemed to burn there like a brand. That pressure on the heart was almost all of which he was conscious — all his being seemed to be centered there, his brain seemed to be paralyzed, and his legs took their steps mechanically as if they were the property of someone else.

The pathway dipped downward at first, before starting its climb to the summit of the Gog Magog hills. As they reached its lowest part the soil became damp, squelching under their shoes, and the stems of the straggly bushes were grey almost to the height of Henry's head, as if spring floods had recently almost covered them. Suddenly Henry noticed with a start of disgust that in the branches of these bushes were several dead rabbits, their fur a dull bluish grey, their eyes blankly staring.

"Look at all these dead rabbits!" he said to Elizabeth. "What do you suppose happened to them?"

"Perhaps they were drowned in the flood."

"Perhaps. But how would they get up in the high branches?"

"Perhaps they were trying to swim on the flood water, and got caught in the branches. Or perhaps someone else came along here, saw the dead rabbits on the ground and threw them up there."

The picture in either case was terrible enough. Or had they, he wondered, been victims of that odd-named disease that wipes out whole populations of rabbits? Mykitosis, or some such name. Had they gone mad and leapt into the branches? There must have been a score of them altogether, limply hanging from the brown branches of the shrubs. It was like a plague.

The children didn't seem to notice the dead rabbits, but went on playing their games of tag and hide and seek.

The path began to climb the hill now, and the bushes grew less frequent. Often there were quite wide clearings on both sides of the path, and it began to seem more like the remains of a Roman road. Henry tried to visualize the road as it must once have been, with grey files of Roman soldiers marching grimly from Colchester to Leicester. He could see their helmets and their shields, hear the tread of their boots and the clanking of their swords. To the natives they must have seemed like strange creatures from another world, so fierce and grimly efficient, symbolizing the death of the old, easy order.

"Look, daddy!"

Helen, the twelve year old, was calling — and pointing to a curious brown blob in the middle of a neighbouring field. What was it? It looked like some furry animal, but its shape was indistinct — it might only be a dead bush or an old stump.

The other children came running over to Helen. "Let's investigate," said Bill, and he started to run across the field towards the curious brown shape. The other children ran after him, and Henry followed more slowly, his feet sinking slightly into the damp turf.

He watched as the children ran ahead of him. When they got near the shape on the ground, something small and furtive suddenly wheeled away and ran swiftly across the field. What was it? Not a rabbit — it was too small for that. A weasel — yes, the flash of its yellow-white underbelly told him that. But there was still something on the ground where the weasel had been. The four children were suddenly quiet, shocked into silence. As he came up to them, he saw what the remaining shape was — a rabbit, still alive and twitching in agony, its throat a raw wound where the weasel had been sucking its blood. The rabbit's eyes were horrible with fear and the knowledge of death.

"Kill it, daddy!" Bill said. "Put it out of its agony. What can we use?"

"Look for a stone," said Henry. "If I had a stone I could kill it."

Glad of something to do, the children scattered and started looking for stones. Henry himself found one first — a big chunk of flint such as in common in East Anglia. He couldn't bring himself to look at the rabbit as he crushed its skull with one strong blow of the stone — he shut his eyes as the blow went home, but he felt the sickening crunch of the tiny skull beneath his hand.

They went back to the road and continued to climb the hill. There was more of a view now — the shrubbery had almost disappeared, and all around you could see the haphazard oblongs of the slightly rolling green and brown fields, divided by hawthorn hedgerows. Elizabeth kept stopping and cupping her eyes to look at the view. Henry knew the signs — she was thinking of doing a painting. He wasn't surprised when she said, "You people go ahead. I think I'll stop and try to do a watercolour." She unfolded her camp stool and sat down, opening up the large watercolour pad that she had been carrying under her arm and getting her paints and waterbottle out of the large handbag into which she had packed her painting supplies and their picnic lunch.

The children and Henry went forward, the children, the death of the rabbit now apparently all but forgotten, once again bounding and leaping and uttering shrill bursts of laughter as they collided or dodged one another in excited play.

"Look, daddy!" said Bill, pointing to a black patch of earth beside the path. "That's where we Scouts had our camp fire! Perhaps we can eat our picnic here on the way back."

"Oh good," said Helen. "What are we having for our picnic?"

"We've brought some hot dogs as usual," said Henry.

"That's good. And what's for dessert?"

"We can roast some marshmallows."

"Great. I could eat right now. But we'd better get to the top of the hill first." And off Helen ran up the path, John and Jane at her heels and Bill trotting along behind at a dignified distance.

Henry turned from watching the children and looked back the way they had come. He expected to be able to see Elizabeth, but the path had twisted and turned without his noticing it and his wife was hidden from sight. He stood for a moment looking over the straggling fields, trying to locate the dead rabbit — but it too was lost to sight. The memory of the raw wound at its throat was not lost, though, nor the sickening sensation of its collapsing skull. And then he felt again that wound in his own chest, the burning weight that pressed through his shirt pocket. The grey-green landscape mirrored his mood, its mess of irregular fields as choatic as his own mind.

Wearily he began the final climb to the summit. He could hear the children's laughter from the wood that ran along the crest of the hill, but their gaiety only heightened his own sadness. How could the children be so unfeeling? How could they laugh and shout on such a day? Children are really savages, he thought, they care for nothing but their own immediate whims.

Suddenly they were all four around him, waving in their hands great bunches of violets.

"Look what we found in the woods, daddy!"

"Look at the flowers."

"That wood is just thick with violets."

"You can pick a bunch like this in just a minute."

"Come and see. There are just millions of them."

He followed the children into the wood — and there they were, under the tall oaks and elms, a great mass of violets forming, amidst the leaves of last autumn, a grey and purple carpet soft to the feet.

"Pick some, daddy!"

"No — don't pick any more. I like to see them on the ground." He didn't want to pull anything from the earth — it had been enough for him today to have killed the rabbit. But the sight of all the violets did please him — for the first time since the message had come he found himself responding pleasurably to his surroundings. He bent down and smelled the flowers — when he got close to the blossoms he could smell their sweet sharp scent, and it reminded him of his wife's perfume. He wondered how her painting was progressing, and he suddenly felt a strong surge of love for her. He was sure that she had stayed behind to paint at least partly so that he could be alone with his thoughts, would not have to make conversation. She was so good, he thought, so undemanding, so ready to find beauty even in the most unpromising scene. He could imagine her patiently brushing the watery paint over her sketch-pad, doing it so seemingly randomly but with such subtle skill and purpose.

The children were having a quiet spell, as if their circuitous climb of the hill had temporarily exhausted their energies. They were all four sitting on the dry leaves of the forest floor, Bill whittling a piece of stick with his pocketknife, Helen arranging her violets into a more graceful bouquet, John searching amid the fallen leaves for bugs, and Jane counting her violets by two's.

Suddenly there was a cracking of branches, and from the thick shrubbery that surrounded the clearing a young couple emerged, holding hands and looking rather sheepish. Henry knew from their appearance that they had been making love — they both looked flushed and triumphant, and yet slightly embarrassed. They nodded and strolled off down the path, hand in hand. The children paid little attention to the lovers, but went on quietly with their own pursuits. Henry watched the young couple out of sight, watched them with warm approval — he could remember when he and Elizabeth had made love among violets, though not in this wood.

"Well" said Helen, "*That* should make a pretty bunch for mother!" And she held up her bouquet of violets, beautifully arranged. "And don't you think it's about time we started to make our picnic?"

"Oh you, Helen," said Bill, "don't you ever think about anything except your stomach?"

"Well I'm hungry, too," said Jane.

"And what about you, John?" Henry asked.

John was still busy at his favourite hobby, catching insects. He didn't seem to hear the question.

Henry repeated it. "Aren't you hungry, John?"

"Oh, I suppose I could eat. But there are lots of bugs in these leaves. I wish I had a jar to put them in."

"Well, come on then, children. Let's look for mother, and if she's ready we'll have our picnic."

"O.K. And look — the sun's coming out for it!" said Helen. And sure enough the haze had thinned to let some pale sunlight through, and the faint rays lit up the shy faces of the violets.

In the warm afternoon sunshine they hurried down the pathway. It seemed a very long way indeed before they came to Elizabeth — but there she was, sitting patiently as Henry had expected, still busily at work on her painting.

"Is the painting finished?" Henry called.

"Just about. I can finish it off in a minute."

The children rushed up to her and looked. "Oh, that's beautiful," said Helen. "That's one of your very best!"

Henry looked over his wife's shoulder at the painting. It *was* beautiful. Elizabeth had subtly arranged the colours and contours of the fields, shrubs and trees into a harmony that you grasped the moment you looked at the painting a harmony which only she had seen in the landscape itself. With a few swift strokes of her brush she finished it, closed her paintbox, stood up and folded her stool.

They walked the short distance to the black patch of earth where the Scouts had had their campfire. While Elizabeth unpacked the food, Henry and the children gathered dry sticks to make a fire. When they had a pile of sticks ready, Henry suddenly realized that he had not brought along any newspaper to start the fire.

"Did you bring any paper to light the fire?" he asked Elizabeth.

"Oh, I'm sorry — no, I didn't think of it."

Then he thought of the telegram in his shirt pocket. With some dry leaves and twigs, it might be enough to get the fire going.

He heaped together some dead leaves beneath the sticks, then pulled the telegram from his pocket and lit it. As it started to burn the flame lit up the words: "Mother died this evening. Dad." Completely unexpected, and he three thousand miles away from her! The leaves caught fire and blazed up — the paper was only a black film of ash. The sticks caught fire, and soon the fire was going strong and the children began to roast their weiners.

The late afternoon sun shone wanly over the pale fields, over the blue-grey corpses in the tangled branches, over the ghostly files of Roman soldiers, over the rabbit with the crushed skull, over the young lovers hand in hand, over the family squatting by the blazing fire. The ache was still in Henry's chest, but it was bearable now, on the Roman road.

The Test

Another disappointing summer. They had had such high hopes in the spring — and then, on threshing day, four hundred and fifty bushels! None of the neighbours did much better, but they had reserves from other years. The Beldings' bins had been absolutely empty — for the last week or two before the threshing they had had to throw sheaves to the hens — and now they were less than half full.

The only thing to do was to keep going. They would have to feed those four hundred pullets anyway, and since they didn't have enough grain of their own they would have to buy some. But where would the money come from? If they only could get on the milk, and have a cheque coming in regularly each month, they might manage it. But that seemed hopeless. She'd spoken to Dickson about it again last week, on her way in to town to market with the eggs, but he'd been no more encouraging than usual. Everything was against you when you were new in the district.

Well, at least they would have a silo this winter. That would help out a bit with the grain — the cows wouldn't need quite so much chop. Whenever Tom could spare time from getting the wheat ground manured and cultivated, he worked at the silo. Gradually it rose higher and higher, its upright cylinder stretching up and up until, at last, it rose above the level of the barn roof. Its steady rise fascinated her; she watched it all day long from the pantry window. It became a symbol for her, a symbol of their determination to survive. Its straight upward thrust to the sky expressed their defiance of whatever forces sought to defeat them.

The usual fall work proceeded. Tom sowed the wheat, the neighbours came and helped fill the silo, most of the ploughing was done. It looked as if they could settle down to waiting out the winter, hoping again that spring and summer would bring a thousand bushel crop.

And then quite unexpectedly one morning as she was hanging out the wash, Dickson drove up in his truck.

"Morning, Mrs. Belding," he called in his hearty way. "How's things today?"

"Oh, busy as usual," she said.

"Never knew a farmer that wasn't," he said. "Like to be busier?"

"Busier? You're not trying to sell us more cows, are you? We've more than we can feed now."

"Oh, I thought maybe with that new silo and all you'd be branching out into a bigger herd."

"Not with the price we get for butter."

It was an obvious hint to prod him into getting them on the milk route, but he ignored it. "How'd those cows turn out I sold you in the spring?"

"Not too badly, I guess. Tom says one of the Holsteins is starting to dry up already, though."

"What about the Jersey?"

"She gives lots of milk, I guess, but Tom says she's an awful hard milker. Takes him twice as long as the others. He's out in the barn till all hours."

"You're getting a fair lot of milk, though?"

"Fair, I guess. Why?"

"Enough for two cans a day?"

He looked her full in the face with a queer sort of smile around his mouth and eyes. It took her a minute to guess what he was getting at. "Two cans ...? You mean there's a chance for us to start shipping?"

"Maybe. If you care to, of course. Maybe you have too much to do. It's lots of work, shipping whole milk you know."

"But of course we care to. Never mind the work. How did it happen? Why, it's only last week you said there wasn't a chance."

"I know. A lot can happen in a week. Reuben Wells up the road is selling out. Figures he's been farming long enough. There's a two-can contract for somebody. You folks is right on the route of the truck, so I'm giving you first chance."

It was all she could do to speak, but she did her best to make her voice sound natural. "Go and ask Tom. He's still in the barn, I think. I feel sure he'll say yes, but you'd better speak to him."

He started across the grass towards the barn, then paused and turned towards her again. "It'll mean a lot of work, you know. You'll have to clean up the barn, build a milkhouse, have the whole place passed by the inspector from Toronto. And the cows will have to be tested too. Can't take any chances on getting T.B. into the city."

"Oh, don't worry about that," she said. "The cows are healthly enough. And as for the work, just tell us what to do and we'll do it if it kills us."

Dickson grinned and went off to the barn to look for Tom. Elizabeth began to hang up the washing again. On the milk at last! She could hardly contain herself for joy. She felt like dancing around the lawn, throwing the clothes in the air, turning somersaults like a child. To get a cheque regularly every month, for twice the amount she could make selling butter on the market, and to be rid of the nuisance of separating, storing cream and churning butter!

Well, it hadn't taken Tom long to make up his mind. Here was Dickson coming out of the barn, and Tom behind him, his face bright and smiling.

"I think Tom's going to start putting up the milkhouse right this minute," Dickson called out to her.

"Yes, where do you think we'd better put it?" Tom stopped by the pump on the lawn. "Somewhere about here, eh? Then we can pump the cold water right into the vats."

The two men began discussing the best site, pacing off the distances, talking in technical terms which she didn't understand. She watched them proudly.

After a few minutes Dickson began to get into his truck. She joined Tom beside the cab.

"When do we start shipping?" she asked.

"Just as soon as you can get ready." he said. "It won't be for a week or two, likely. But Tom knows what to do now, and as soon as he lets me know he's ready I'll arrange for the inspector to come out."

He pressed the starter and the engine roared in response. He backed it around in the driveway, waved at them both, and was off.

She turned to Tom. "Isn't it wonderful?" she said. "I can hardly believe it yet, can you?"

Instead of answering, he took her in his arms and they stood for several minutes in a close embrace. "Well, this won't do," he said at last. "I'd better get the team out and finish that ploughing. Once that's done I can get at the barn and milkhouse."

That night after he had finished the milking Tom drew a sketch of the milkhouse and calculated the amount of lumber and shingles and paint and cement he would need. Next morning he walked over the nearest neighbour's place and phoned in an order for the supplies. That done, he started on the barn. With an old broom he swept down the cobwebs from the corners, brushed the dust from the beams and walls and floors. Then he got a washboiler full of hot water, put in some disinfectant, and washed every surface by hand. He had to leave it then, to dry, but first thing next morning he mixed up some whitewash and sprayed the whole inside of the barn until it was white and shining.

He called Elizabeth into the barn to inspect his work. "How does it look?"

She could hardly believe her eyes. She had never realized before how dark and dismal a place the barn had been: now it was bright and dazzlingly clean. "What a place for cows!" she said. "Why, I wouldn't mind eating my own meals in here."

"Do you think it will pass the inspector?" he asked, so seriously that she had to laugh at him.

"Of course it will," she said. "Why I'll bet there isn't as clean a barn in Barfoot Station."

Meanwhile the lumber and other supplies had arrived from town, and he began on the milkhouse. His energy amazed her — and his skill. She had never seen him work so hard in their two years of married life, and she had never known before that he was so clever with tools. One of the neighbours came over and helped him with some of the heaviest work, but he built the milkhouse from his own plans and almost entirely with his own hands. And it was well designed, too, and well built. It neatly filled the space between the pump and the fence separating the lawn from the barnyard, and its proportions were pleasing. With the new silo and the new milkhouse, things were beginning to look a lot better around the place, in spite of the poor seasons they had had.

The inspector came from Toronto, and was delighted with the barn and the milkhouse. Now if only the cows turned out to be free from T.B., they would be all set! She had taken it as a matter of course that the cows were healthy, but now that he was actually testing them she began to wonder. You heard such queer things about these tests... Suppose one or two of the best cows went down, and they weren't able to fill the two cans? They just couldn't afford to buy more cows, what with the silo still to be paid for, and the grain to buy.

When the inspector came from the barn after administering the test, she searched his face anxiously. "Do you think they're all right?" she asked.

"Oh, I feel sure they'll be all right," he smiled. Then he looked at her more seriously. "But of course, you never can tell. The healthiest looking cows sometimes turn out to be riddled with T.B. But don't you worry about it. Mr. Belding's made a grand job of the barn and milkhouse, and I think you can count on being on the milk in another week's time. I'll let you know the results of the tests just as soon as I can."

He went off in his car, and she was left to wonder. In spite of what he had said, she couldn't help worrying. She went into the barn herself, and looked at the cows. Apart from the old Jersey, who was always thin, the cows certainly looked healthy. Their ribs were well covered with flesh in spite of the scanty pastures they had fed on all summer. And then as she watched, one of the Holsteins they had bought from Dickson in the spring, the one which Tom said was already going dry, lifted its black and white head and uttered a long cough. It was a dry, hollow cough which made her shudder and made the brightly whitewashed barn suddenly seem grey and terrifying.

Where was Tom? She found him in the toolshed, fixing some broken harness. "What's the matter, honey?" he said. "You look kinda scared."

"That Holstein we got from Dickson," she said, "you know, the one that's going dry — she coughed when I was in the barn. Does she cough a lot?"

"I've never noticed her, specially," said Tom. "A cow'll often cough, if she gets a bit of dust or something in her throat. That's likely all it was. I fed them a forkful of the hay left over from last year. It's pretty dusty stuff by now."

That cough worried her, nevertheless. It was something on which her anxiety could fasten, and it stuck there in her throat through all the days of waiting for the inspector to return. She kept going out to the barn to sneak a look at the cows, never letting on to Tom that she was doing it, and though she only heard the cough once again it was enough to keep her fears alive.

Finally the inspector's car appeared. As soon as she recognized it she ran out of the house to the lawn. She went over to the side of the car, but the inspector scarcely looked at her. He merely nodded a greeting, and did not speak to her until he had got out of the car and was standing beside her on the lawn. Then, looking not at her but at the barn, he blurted it out. "I'm afraid I have bad news for you, Mrs. Belding."

Her heart jumped, seemed to turn over, and began to pound. "Bad news?" she said. "Some of the cows went down?"

He nodded.

"How many?"

He was still looking towards the barn, and shifting uneasily from foot to foot. He took a long time to answer. At last he said, "Mrs. Belding, I hate to tell you this, but you'll have to know it sooner or later. Your whole herd went down."

"All of them?" She felt as if she must fall. There was no strength in her. It was as if her real self had left her body, which stood a mere shell, miraculously erect. All of them! Even in her most anxious moments she had never even imagined that they all might go down. One or two perhaps, even the three new ones from Dickson, but not them all.

Still her body remained upright, and by degrees it seemed that she took possession of it again. She held taut the muscles of her face. This man must not see how much it meant to her. Her voice was tense but controlled as she asked, "Then we can't ship milk?"

"I'm afraid not. I'm very sorry. But there's nothing I can do about it." He glanced at her for the first time and attempted a smile. Then, as he looked again towards the barn, he repeated the word "nothing" as if he had searched his mind in vain for comfort.

"Are you sure of the test? Could there have been some mistake?" Her mind was beginning to function again. She remembered stories she had heard, especially one of a cow that had been tested and passed as sound and then had died of the disease a few months later. "They say," she said, made bold by her desperation, "that the test is not always reliable."

He looked at her quietly, apparently not irritated by her doubt. "I'm afraid there's no chance of a mistake," he said. "If it had been the other way... Sometimes a cow that has a disease will show no reaction. But when the reaction occurs, we know the disease is there."

Well, there it was then. Hard, ugly, unchangeable. Their whole herd was diseased.

The inspector got into his car and drove off. She went into the house. Now that there was no one to see her she let herself go and cried bitterly, in hard sobs that tore at her chest and throat. When she had cried herself out, she sat on the sofa by the dining-room window and looked out over the fields. It was a grey day in early November. The trees had lost their leaves, and the fields were brown and damp and bare. This was the end, the dirty stub of the year, the dreary close of their struggle. It was no use trying to go on. Everything was against them. She had no more energy to fight back.

Farming! What a life! No wonder Reuben Wells was selling out. That is what Tom and she had better do, before their youth and hope were utterly destroyed, withered by the droughts and blasted by the winds.

She couldn't stand it indoors any longer. She felt that she would suffocate or go mad unless she got out into the fresh air.

She put on the old hat and coat she wore to feed the chickens and went out into the yard. She walked across the lawn, through the gate leading into the barn, into the barn itself. There were the cows, staring curiously at her, looking as healthy as ever. She hated them, hated their great stupid staring eyes and their ugly snuffing nostrils.

She went outside again, walked down into the apple orchard and looked back at the barn. There was the silo, standing beside the barn, stuffed full of corn. A great deal of good to them it was now, with a barn full of tubercular cows. She sat down on the stump of an old apple tree which had been destroyed by the ice-storm last winter. She kept her eyes on the silo. Gradually as she stared at it she began to feel again the symbolic quality of its structure, the challenging defiance of its erect cylindrical climb.

She sat on the stump a long time. Miraculously she could feel slowly gathering in herself reserves of will that she had thought to be drained and empty. Was she really ready to give in, to surrender thus easily to disaster? No. She wanted to fight back, to match the proud defiance of the silo rearing to the sky. But how could she fight? What could she do? The inspector had obviously wanted to help, but he could think of nothing.

It seemed at least an hour that she sat there on the stump, the sweet smell of fallen apples about her and the dull grey sky above her head. There must be something they could do!

She jumed up at last, and began to hurry towards Tom who was running the furrows in the last ploughed field. She passed the barn and the tall silo and started up the lane. She passed the small hickory trees at the corner, and walked underneath the bare branches of the huge elms which bordered the lane. She came at last to the field where Tom was, and waited for him to come to the headland.

"Tom," she blurted out, forgetting that he had not heard the news, "can you get anything at all for cows with T.B.?"

"If they're not too badly gone, you can. You can sell them for canners and cutters, but you don't get much. Why? You're not really expecting ours to go down, are you? That cough doesn't mean anything. Any cow'll cough on dry dusty hay."

"They have gone down."

His face turned white and his hands clenched. "Has the inspector been?"

She nodded. "He was here an hour or so ago."

"How many?"

"All of them. The whole herd."

He stood as she had stood when the inspector told her, as if in a trance. "That's it, then," he said dully, all the enthusiasm of the last two weeks gone from his voice and his face.

"That's the way I felt, Tom, an hour ago. But I've been thinking. Couldn't we sell these grade cows for beef, as you say, and make a start on the pure-bred herd we've been longing for?"

"But pure-breds are expensive. We couldn't get more than two or three for all nine of the grades."

"All right. We'll get along for a while with fewer. They'll have calves after a while, and we can build the herd up. At least we'll know what we're getting."

It was too much for him to take in all at once. They talked it over back and forth for a long time. Gradually she pumped into him her own will to survive. "You know," he said finally, "Dickson might even give us credit on two or three extra pure-breds, now we're on the milk and all. He'd know we'd pay him back." Suddenly his face brightened. "Yes, and there'll be the government compensation for the cows that went down. I'd forgotten that. Yes, we'll have enough for a good start on a pure-bred herd."

When they were talked out he went back on his work on the furrows, and she waited for him at the headland. When the sun began to set, and it was time for him to start the chores and for her to get supper ready, they walked down the lane together towards the clean barn and the full silo.

The Mirror

It was a rush to get everything ready for the party, but by eight-thirty the baby was quiet and the living-room tidy. While Elizabeth was putting the finishing touches to her make-up in the bedroom, Bill straightened his hair and tie at the long mirror in the downstairs hall. It was not a bad-looking face, he decided, at least not in this light.

The bell rang. It was Kate Hall. She bounced in, and danced a little circular pirouette which unwound her fur jacket into his waiting hands.

She flopped into the big green easy chair by the fireplace, clasped her black taffeta skirt about her smooth knees, and looked up at him expectantly. As usual, there was something about her look which baffled him. Somehow her upthrust chin, her parted lips, and her bright, bold eyes conveyed a mixture of friendliness and detachment, of appreciation and mockery. He didn't know whether she was expecting him to say something clever, or daring him to say anything which she wouldn't regard as dull.

He always felt like this in her company. He was socially insecure anyway, always a trifle ill at ease with people other than his wife, but with Kate he was especially wary. There was no real basis for it, he thought as he lit her cigarette and ventured another look into her eyes, for she had never been anything but kind to him and Elizabeth. She was, in fact, much their best friend here, the person who more than anyone else had welcomed them and made them feel at home in this small, raw Western Canadian town.

Perhaps that was partly the trouble — that they owed her so much, were so dependent on her. If it hadn't been for Kate Hall, this first winter would have been intolerable. It was she who had been the first to call on them, and to invite them into her home. And when she found that Bill tried to write, and Elizabeth to draw, and that they were both interested in the theatre, she had treated them as enthusiastically as if they were already artists of acknowledged genius.

Being thus adopted by Kate had meant being automatically adopted by her circle of friends — and a good circle it was, by any standards, and superlatively good by standards one had a right to apply in a town of this size and location. Her friends were all young professional people like themselves — other teachers on the High School staff, a young doctor and his wife, a couple of lawyers, a music teacher, the two social workers. They met regularly each week, in one another's homes, usually to read plays, sometimes simply to chat or play games.

But it was Kate who held the circle together: you knew that if she left town the group would disintegrate. She dominated it and yet you couldn't call her domineering. She usually cast the plays, but she cast them tactfully, varying the leads from evening to evening and never seeking to steal the limelight herself.

And yet Bill felt uneasy, suspicious. It was as if her tremendous enthusiasm, her overflowing vitality, concealed a cold, sharp, steel centre, as if at any moment her energy, creative and spontaneous as it seemed, might become deliberately destructive.

But how absurb of him, he thought, as she said innocently, "Any bright ideas for tonight, Bill?"

"Plays, you mean?"

"No. Let's not read a play this week. That last Ibsen left a bad taste in my mouth."

"What then?"

"Let's have fun. Games."

"*The* Game?"

"If you like. I thought of a beauty on the way over. Nobody would *ever* get it."

"Can you tell me?"

"No. Too good to give away — even to you. But I don't feel like The Game tonight. Too much work. Any other ideas?"

"Guggenheim?"

"That's even more work."

"We needn't play it pure. Then it's easy. Say — I have an idea."

Her face brightened and she looked at him with an almost adoring expression. What a fool he was to doubt her! But adoring — now he was going to the other extreme. It was time he got over these ridiculous alternations of his ego from exaltation to abasement. Why couldn't he accept himself as he was, as a fairly bright young man of slightly more than average talent, instead of either trying to puff himself up into a genius or whittle himself down to a fool? Why couldn't he suggest a game as casually as anyone else would, instead of imagining that whatever he said would stamp him either as a hero or a goat?

Forcing himself to sound casual, he said, "It's a game we played last summer in Winnipeg."

"How does it go?"

"It's really just a special version of Personalities. Instead of picking anyone from anywhere, you pick someone local, someone everybody knows. You begin with faint clues, and go on making them stronger until somebody guesses. Then it's their turn."

"Sounds easy enough. Just the kind of game I feel like." She looked thoughtful for a moment. He wondered if, after all, he had displeased her, if the brilliant idea he had led her to expect had proved disappointingly dull. But no — her face was eager again. "Yes," she said. "I like it. I can see all sorts of possibilities."

Elizabeth came down then, and while she was apologizing to Kate for being late the doorbell rang again. It rang almost continuously for the next five minutes as the rest of the gang trooped in, threw their coats on the couch in the study, and took their places in a rough semi-circle around the fire.

When they were all settled comfortably, Kate suggested that they skip the play-reading for once and try Bill's game. Everyone was agreeable — they usually were, to Kate's suggestions — and they began.

Marion Macdonald, the French teacher at the High School, was given the first turn, and did an amusing sketch of the bishop of the local diocese. Pat McArdle, wife of the doctor, drew a lively satirical portrait of her husband.

Now it was Kate's turn. She was at her most vivacious, sitting on the edge of her chair, her hands moving in rapid, jerky gestures, her eyes flashing with excitement. Everyone's interest perked up: Kate could be depended upon to be devastatingly funny at somebody's expense.

Bill, however, felt a momentary revulsion as he looked at her. She's like some rapacious bird, he thought, her fingernails sharp claws ready to tear the flesh from some innocent victim. He saw the lamb quiver, seek the ewe's side, as the eagle poised and swooped. He wished he hadn't suggested the game. It was really just a slightly refined form of malicious gossip.

But it was too late now. Kate had already started. He had missed her first clues, but now he forced himself to listen. "He's clever, but he's not half as clever as he thinks he is. He's a small frog in a small puddle, but he acts like a toad in a hole. Deep down he knows he hasn't a shred of talent, but he scarcely even admits it to himself and never to anyone else. He thinks he can write, but he couldn't even write a letter that wasn't full of clichés and platitudes. He's the type who never answers the door without first going to the mirror and congratulating himself on his good looks."

Bill winced. How could she have known that about him? The whole atmosphere of the room seemed to have changed from easy, bantering informality to a strained and baffled embarrassment. Bill could feel the tension in every muscle of his body, and especially in his face and neck. He gripped his hands into tight knots and tried to look calm. He kept his eyes focused on Kate's face, which seemed to have lost all its warm vitality and to have become a mask of settled ferocity. He dared not look at the others, but he felt all their eyes were on him.

The words continued to come from Kate's mouth like the sharp strokes of a whip — "the epitome of vanity and self-importance... a gift of the gab which he confounds with eloquence... an ambition that makes Macbeth seem humble."

The tension mounted, wave upon wave that flowed up and down the nerves of his skin. What could he do? He had known that sometime the cold steel behind that warm exterior would break out into violence, had suspected that some day it would be turned against himself, but never in his worst imaginings had he forseen this. To be attacked — that he had feared, even in a sense expected, but not to be attacked so publicly, so bitterly, and so long.

What could he say or do that would break the tension? Whatever he did, it would mean the end of the group. No group could survive a strain of this sort. Should he admit that and walk out now, walk into the cold brilliance of the February night and come back only when the rest had made their apologies and left?

She was still going on, piling on the insults until the weight of them seemed physically to oppress him. The others did nothing but giggle now and then with embarrassment. Why for God's sake didn't somebody say something, stop her, give him some peace? Were they going to let her torture him all night? If somebody didn't name him soon he'd shout it out himself, say, "*All right. You've seen through me. You've pinned me to the wall. I'm everything you say and more. But did you have to tell me at my own party, in my own house, before all the friends I have?*"

The words were struggling somewhere in the choked muscles of his throat when he heard a voice almost scream the name "George Bellamy!"

He felt nothing for a moment, then a vast deflation as if he were a balloon suddenly punctured.

Everybody else was saying, "Bellamy! Of course! The one person Kate really despises. Why didn't we think of him? How stupid? I couldn't think of a soul."

At last Bill dared to glance around at the faces of his friends. Everybody else looked relaxed and happy. They had been baffled, the solution had come, and they were pleased. Nothing more than that. Kate loked especially happy — she had purged herself of malice, and had stumped her friends. No one had even thought of him, and he'd been so sure. They hadn't even noticed his tension, apparently, for there was Elizabeth, who would have been, sure to notice first, grinning at him as she said, "Well, Bill and I had a good excuse, for we've never met this Bellamy. Who is he?"

"Oh," said the doctor, "Don't you know him? Manager of the radio station. Kate hates him because he'll never give the Little Theatre any radio time. And he *is* a conceited ass."

The game went on, while Bill felt the air flow ever so gently back into the pricked balloon of his ego.

By the time the guests were leaving, Bill felt sufficiently recovered to ask, "What's the programme for next week, Kate?"

She smiled at him, friendly as ever, and without even a hint of mockery in her expression. "We've had our fun — now it's back to business. *Pillars of Society,* my lad — and there's a perfect part in it for you."

The guests trooped out together, chorusing goodnights. "We haven't had such fun in years." "What a party!"

Elizabeth hurried into the living-room and started to clear up the cups. Bill lingered in the hall, started to look in the long mirror but turned away in disgust. No, that would never do. He turned back to the mirror and had a good long hard look at himself.

The Trespasser

He walked quickly along the road towards the entrance of the rectory, checking his new watch every few seconds to make sure that he would arrive on time, but when he came to the big white wooden gate he had a moment of terror, and stopped with his hand on the heavy iron latch.

Beyond the gate was a world of which he knew little, though for weeks he had dreamed of it. He had dreamed of it as a paradise which he would never be allowed to enter, and now that he was about to open the gate he felt guilty as a trespasser. It had no forbidding sign, no blunt excluding TRESPASSERS WILL BE PROSECUTED, but it was the kind of gate that did have such signs. Yes, that was it, he decided, it was merely the habit of passing by such gates and believing that he must always be doomed to pass them that made him hesitate.

But there was another feeling mingled with it, he realized, his hand still on the unlifted latch. He wanted desperately to enter and yet he was afraid, afraid that the garden, the house would prove unworthy of his dreams. Once he had entered, the dream would be over. What would take its place? He shrank from knowledge even as he yearned for it.

He glanced again at his watch. If he was going in, he must do so now. The invitation had said tea would be served at four, and he had only a minute in which to walk up the driveway. Even yet he could scarcely believe that the invitation, written in an elaborate looping hand that he took to be Mrs. Cooper's, had actually been meant for him. He pulled it from his pocket and read it for the hundredth time, remembering the moment when the postman had brought it and the way his mother had said, "Well, you *are* getting up in the world! Hm! Well, they might have had the decency to invite me too. I suppose I'm not good enough for them."

He gathered together all his resolution — it was a real physical effort, as if he were catching hold of loose strings of himself and tying them together — and lifted the latch. The big gate, perfectly hung on oiled hinges, swung open at a touch, and he went through into the garden. He closed the gate cautiously, and stood inside almost trembling, as he had stood that first day he, the "new boy", entered the Headmaster's study. At a sound, a sudden movement, he would have bolted like a rabbit; but nothing stirred in the garden. It was as quiet and still as if he had indeed by some miracle wandered back into the First Garden and found it as it was after Adam and Eve had left it. Struck with the fancy, he looked for the forbidden tree but saw only elms and apple trees, their leaves and branches poised like enchanted dancers.

He began to walk quickly but cautiously, the crisp gravel crunching under his feet. Around a curve of the tree-lined driveway he came suddenly upon the house. It was even grander, statelier than he had imagined. The shutters, window frames and doors were a dazzling white; thick dark green ivy clung to the red brick walls. Between the driveway and the house were flower-beds bordered by thin strips of grass, and on either side were thick smooth lawns dotted with symmetrical shrubs. All was order, innocence, peace; he felt like an intruder as he lifted the shining brass knocker and startled the silence with his rapping.

A trim little maid, correct as a penguin, opened the door.

"I am Mr. Hunt..." George said timidly, wondering whether in so doing he had made a social blunder. Should he have said "Master Hunt"? But that always made him giggle; it sounded as if he were a master of foxhounds. Perhaps "George Hunt" would have been best?

"Oh yes," the maid said, with a smile that might have been friendly or mocking, "come in, sir. Mrs. Cooper is expecting you."

Sir! That smile! Was she making fun of him? He blushed and stepped inside awkwardly. He had a quick glimpse of dark panelled walls and polished floors, then found himself in a large bright room to the left of the hall.

The rector came forward and greeted him. "Mother," he said to the lady who sat stately as a goddess by the window, "this is George Hunt. George, my mother, Mrs. Cooper."

George bowed awkwardly in her direction. "Pleased to meet you," he muttered, and immediately remembered that his mother had told him not to acknowledge introductions in that way. He blushed again and stood twisting his battered school cap in his hands.

The goddess rose, taller than her son, and came towards him. She seemed to him to swim suspended in the cool scented air while he, awkward as a crab, twisted helpless on the sandy ocean floor.

"Of course," she said, "Mr. Hunt! May I can call you George? I've heard so *much* about you. So many *nice* things, of course. From my son. He's been delighted to have you in Lanton this summer, simply delighted. A real *find*."

He felt himself drowned in the waves of her words. He stood still stupidly twisting the cap, and she must have noticed for she said: "Ah, what a lovely cap! What is your school?"

He mumbled the name, acutely conscious that it was not a "good" school, but merely a residential grammar school in a small provincial town. He held the cap out for her better inspection.

"Crampton?" she said. "It's a nice name, and a nice cap. It must be a good school, though I must admit I haven't heard of it. But I have no memory for these things. John would know... He was at Rugby, of course."

The rector came to the rescue. "I suppose you'd like to get rid of that cap," he said. "Just hang it on the tree in the hall."

Glad of the excuse to escape momentarily, but sure that he had blundered in bringing the cap into the drawingroom, he did as suggested.

The maid brought in the tea, and with cup and scones to occupy his hands he began to feel better. Gradually he found himself losing his fear of Mrs. Cooper. She seemed so genuinely interested in him.

"John tells me you have a lovely voice," she said. "You've made all the difference to the choir. I'm so fond of boy sopranos. I wish I could get to church more often, but no one keeps carriages nowadays, and I can't bear the smell of petrol. I get a headache every time I go near a motorcar. But we must talk about *you*. Are you a trained singer?"

"Mother gave me all the training I've had. She has a wonderful voice, and used to do a great deal of singing."

"Did she sing—er, professionally?"

"She could have sung professionally, but her mother wouldn't let her."

"So she took up nursing instead?"

"Yes."

"And do you always spend your holidays where she is working — nursing, I mean?"

"Yes."

"What a nice idea. You must see a lot of England."

"Yes. You know, it's funny. Last summer we were in Cambridgeshire — and here we are now near Oxford!"

"Isn't that a coincidence? I'm sure you like Oxfordshire better. Cambridge is such a damp place, near those Fens, and so flat and dull. Was your mother near Cambridge long?"

"About two years."

"I suppose she likes to move around. Was she happy there?"

"Oh yes, very happy. But it was a big, heavy district, and she wanted something easier."

"Well I do hope she'll stay here. We've wanted a really good nurse for so long. The villagers are very fond of your mother already, and she seems *such* a lady. The last nurse was really quite *common*. But it must be a difficult life for your mother, earning her own living and bringing up a big boy like you. Has your father been dead very long?"

He wavered for a moment, but the stock phrase came out as usual: "Yes. He was killed in the War. When I was a baby."

The conversation flowed on in the cool soft light of the late afternoon, and he floated along in the stream of it, easily, naturally, no longer the awkward crab but the splendid fish lazily swimming. The grandfather clock in the hall leisurely measured off the minutes, softly chimed the quarters and halves. The maid came in and cleared away the tea-things, but still they sat on, the rector absorbed and almost silent, the mother eagerly questioning, the boy pouring out his confidences.

For it seemed to him already that he knew this goddess-like creature better than his own mother, that he could tell her everything, talk to her forever, and that she would always understand. He told her about his mother's people, tenant farmers in the Midlands, and about his father, caught in the War just as he was beginning to make his way as an engineer. He told her about the difficulties his mother had, as a married woman with a child, to find a suitable nursing district. He told her about the skimping and saving his mother did to clothe him properly for school, and about the school itself, the scholarship he had won to get there, that first fearful interview with the solemn Headmaster.

Suddenly, through the calm of the evening dusk, came three dull strokes of a gong. George jumped as if the strokes had been aimed at him. He saw the rector and his mother exchange glances. Mrs. Cooper looked at her watch. "Why, would you believe it?" she said. "That's the dinner gong! It's seven o'clock already! Why, it only seems like a few minutes since you came in."

George jumped up in confusion. He had stayed too long — the very thing his mother had warned him against most strongly! "I'm awfully sorry," he muttered. "I... I didn't realize... Mother will be dreadfully upset."

"Oh, don't hurry away," Mrs. Cooper said. "It has been so pleasant. Will you stay with us for dinner?"

Did she really want him to stay? She seemed to. He looked at the rector, but the rector gave no sign. He thought of his mother's advice, of the fact that she was waiting for him; but the idea of having dinner in this lovely old house with Mrs. Cooper fascinated him. He knew he should leave, but he could not. He tried to gather up the strings of himself as he had at the gate, but his fingers were numb and clumsy.

He stayed for dinner.

At first he sat, dream-wrapped, in the panelled dining-room and glowed with delight. Mrs. Cooper went on eagerly questioning; the rector sat absorbed and almost silent; the penguin-like maid hovered obsequiously around the table.

Slowly the dream dissolved. Thoughts of his mother, anxiously waiting for him in the little nurse's cottage, could no longer be thrust aside. Mrs. Cooper seemed to be losing interest in him; she began to talk more with her son; it was the rector now who spoke to the boy as if he too were aware of the mother's sudden loss of interest. George grew more restless each second; as soon as the meal was over he said good-bye hurriedly, become once more the awkward young boy from the village who had crept miraculously into a world above him.

He dashed out of the front door and began to run down the driveway. His feet crunched loudly in the gravel, disturbing the still-silent garden. But now the garden had an evil, menacing silence; the shrubs were dark and twisted shapes; the trees crouched like savage beasts.

He came at last, gladly, to the gate, opened it awkwardly, twisted through, and carefully, decisively, closed it behind him.

Suddenly, as he reached the safety of the road, he realized that his head was cold in the night air: he had left his cap in the hall! No, he would not go back there for it, for anything. As surely as if he were there, listening, he knew that Mrs. Cooper was now ridiculing him, overcoming the weak defences of the rector, knew that she had pumped him, tempted him, and betrayed him, knew that he would fully deserve his own mother's inevitable contempt.

Aunt Polly

What her real name was I am not sure, for among the family she was always known simply as Aunt Polly. I think that she had been christened Mary Ann, but it is not important. Aunt Polly was the right name for her, for it expressed as no other name could her homely good nature.

Her home in the little Midland town of Collingham was a tiny brick cottage situated on an obscure back street among similar houses of the aged poor. For Aunt Polly belonged to the poor branch of the family, was the sister of my grandmother, and like her had started life as a cook. Grandmother had "bettered herself" by marrying her employer, a gentleman farmer, but Aunt Polly had had to be content with one of the farm-labourers in the village where she worked. To him she had borne six children, and when the children were all still under the age of ten he had died, crushed under an overturned hay-wagon. Then she had moved to the cottage in Collingham and had begun to support herself and the six children by taking in washing and needlework from the homes of the gentry.

All this I knew only by hearsay, from the endless stories of the family which Grandmother poured into my ears as we sat together by the fireplace in the winter evenings. When I first knew Aunt Polly, she was an old lady of seventy, her duties confined to keeping house for her eldest son, Uncle Arthur. Uncle Arthur was a bachelor who worked as a plate-layer on the London, Midland and Scottish Railway. Of her other children, two were dead; one, a married daughter called Aunt Jennie, lived on a farm just beyond Collingham; and the other two, Uncle Fred and Uncle Tom, were coal-miners living in Mansfield about thirty miles away.

It may be that the passing of the years, and especially the successful bringing up of her large family, had mellowed Aunt Polly, and that she had not always been the happy, hearty person whom I as a small boy came to know and love. I hardly think so, however, for Grandmother's portraits of the family were usually flavoured with vinegar, whereas for Aunt Polly she had nothing but kind words and a warm knowing smile which said: "But Aunt Polly now — there is a woman one can only love." Even when the news of her husband's tragic death reached her, Aunt Polly's outward cheerfulness must have clung to her, and I can imagine her smiling reassuringly to the ring of open-mouthed children and saying something warm and comforting to soften the blow.

At any rate, when I knew her forty years after this, she was the very soul of kindness and gaiety. Just to look at her was enough to make one's spirits expand. She was built on ample lines, but her bulk was by no means repulsive for she had the necessary height to give it dignity. To me, a boy of seven when I first met her, she seemed a veritable giantess, and had if not been for her obvious good nature I should have been rather afraid of her.

But to be afraid of Aunt Polly was out of the question. She had a round face, a ruddy complexion usually rendered more striking by the heat from the oven (for she was already baking the most delicious pies and cakes a boy ever tasted), full but not thick lips which stretched into a smile on the slightest occasion, and bright blue eyes which looked out on the world with complete confidence.

What an enchanted land, to the small boy, was the room which served as kitchen, dining-room, and living-room in her tiny cottage! It was full of furniture, brought from the larger home of Aunt Polly's married days, for she refused to part with anything which could remind her of her much-loved husband. Conspicuous were such pieces as excite a child's wonder and curiosity — tall chests of drawers stuffed to overflowing, a corner cupboard laden with china trinkets, and, most exciting of all, a tall grand-father clock which ticked majestically from second to second to the entrancing accompaniment of the swing of the mighty pendulum, and, every quarter hour, pealed out a regular carillon of chimes.

Nor was Aunt Polly jealous of her possessions. Grandmother kept most of her drawers and cupboards locked up, but if Aunt Polly had ever had a key she had long since thrown it away as a needless encumbrance. "Would you like to look through the drawers for treasures, lad?" she would say, her merry face alight. "Go ahead and welcome. You can't hurt anything." And so the delightful hunt would begin. I would dart a hand into a drawer, and pull out, say, a highly ornamented pin-cushion.

"Where did you get this, Aunt Polly?"

"What, child?" she would answer, turning round from the oven. "Oh, that, why, bless your heart, your own grandmother gave me that the first Christmas we were both in service. She was over in Shirebrook, you know, and..." And away she would go on a story of their youth nearly sixty years ago, in the reign of Queen Victoria.

Even the corner cupboard was not forbidden ground. In it were all sorts of occasions for anecdotes: cups and spoons lettered or engraved with the names of seaside resorts like Skegness and Cleethorpes (mementoes of Sunday School excursions to these legendary ports); china objects commemorating the Queen's Jubilee, the coronations of Edward VII and George V; and cheap plated cups and forks which had been given by godparents to Aunt Polly's children. These things were never used; that would be a form of sacrilege. They were not merely *things*, they were alive, living embodiments of the past.

When I grew tired of hunting through the drawers and cupboards there were books to be read. There was a line of books across the top of every chest of drawers. To the boy they were not merely books, but gateways to new worlds. There was *The Pilgrim's Progress*, profusely illustrated with drawings of men and dragons; there were stories of the exploits of missionaries and the sufferings of heroic martyrs in lands whose very names spelt romance; there was the very improving *Eric, or Little by Little*; there were temperance tracts and one particularly sorrowful story, whose title I have forgotten, which chronicled the weary vigil of a mother who for years kept a lamp burning in her window to guide an erring son transported to Australia.

Mournful though some of the books were, they never depressed my spirits, and the memory of their reading is haloed with contentment. Perhaps this is because they all chronicled the ultimate triumph of goodness, but even more is it a tribute to the unfailing cheerfulness of Aunt Polly, in whose comfortable presence even dragons lost their terror.

It was usually in the day time that I visited Aunt Polly. Grandmother would often let me take the four-mile bus ride on Saturdays when there was no school, or during the holidays. But I had to be back before dark, and this meant that I did not see Uncle Arthur. Sometimes, however, Grandmother would go in with me, and we would stay until after supper. On these occasions there would be much merriments, for Uncle Arthur shared his mother's cheerfulness. He was a huge man with a florid face, gingery hair beginning to show traces of grey, and a large drooping moustache which made it necessary for him to drink his tea out of a special moustache cup. The drinking was accompanied by a loud sucking noise, and invariably, on our way home in the bus, Grandmother would warn me not to take Uncle Arthur as a model of table manners. Grandmother was very conscious of her superior social status, and she would say: "Your Uncle Arthur is rather uncouth, but he has a heart of gold. There are many rich men who are not the gentleman he is at heart."

To me, no such defence was necessary. The fact that Uncle Arthur could sing and tell stories more than atoned for his occasional coarseness in speech and manner. He had a powerful bass voice which sent thrills of delight up and down my spine, and he seemed to have an inexhaustible store of songs. He needed no accompaniment. All I had to do was say "Sing me *Tom Bowling* now, Uncle," and he would comply directly. Songs of the sea were his favourites; though his acquaintance with the sea was limited to a few single-day visits to Skegness.

His stories were more closely based upon experience. They fell into two classes: those concerned with his job, railroading; and those relating to his hobby, trapping rabbits. Grandmother rather disapproved of both varieties. The railroad stories told of actual or threatened disasters, and the rabbit-trapping tales centred about poaching. Needless to say, I had no qualms and listened to Uncle Arthur's yarns as eagerly as, on other occasions, I read of the heroic deeds of the knights of his famous namesake.

Aunt Polly's married daughter, Aunt Jennie, I saw infrequently, but twice I spent holiday weekends on her farm. Aunt Jennie was a motherly soul of about forty, and fully shared her mother's generosity. My memory of those weekends consists very largely of huge meals served in the farm kitchen to the accompaniment of laughter. She had two children: Ben, who was about six months my senior, and Rose, who was about two years younger. With them

I went on long rambles through the fields picking blackberries which Aunt Jennie then made into tempting pies, or climbed about the farm buildings in search of bird's nests.

About three years after I first met Aunt Polly a letter arrived for Grandmother written in Uncle Arthur's large uneven scrawl. It was to say that Aunt Polly was not feeling very well. Grandmother at once decided that I should go into Collingham on the first bus to see how serious the illness might be.

I shall never forget that morning. It was in an English November — cold and grey and wet. When the bus reached Collingham the first person I met was Mr. Nicholson, a local draper and a friend of the family. He was a long thin cadaverous man who never smiled. "Good morning, Danny," he said in a mournful tone.

"Good morning, Mr. Nicholson. Have you heard how Aunt Polly is this morning?"

His eyes didn't flicker at all as he replied tonelessly: "She's dead. Heart. In the night."

The words had the breath-taking force of a kick in the stomach. Utterly bewildered, like a cornered animal I looked about for a mode of escape. I caught sight of the bus just starting on its return journey, ran after it, banged on the entrance door, and jumped in to make the journey home.

Three days later Grandmother and I came into Collingham for the funeral. As soon as I entered the cottage I was aware of a change of atmosphere. A fire was burning in the grate, but the room had none of its old warmth. The grandfather clock whose slow regular ticking had seemed so reassuring in earlier days had now taken on a dreary monotone, and its once gay chimes were gay no longer.

All the members of the family were there, but they were scarcely recognizable. Their faces were set in grim formal lines, and they appeared embarrassed in their stiff Sunday clothes. Uncle Arthur had on a black serge suit which smelt strongly of mothballs, and a high wing collar, once white but now a dingy yellow. He was obviously unused to the collar, and kept running his finger inside it in a futile effort to ease the chafing.

There was an awkward pause as we entered, as if the brothers and Aunt Jennie had been discussing something which Grandmother and I should not hear. After she had helped Grandmother off with her coat, and I had hung mine on its usual peg, Aunt Jennie said: "Mother is in here, Aunt Rachel." She pointed to the door of her bedroom. "Will you come in and see her?"

As Grandmother began to follow her, Aunt Jennie looked over at me. "What about you, Danny? Would you like to see your Aunt Polly?"

Scared though I was, it seemed easier to go than to refuse. I have always regretted going. Now, whenever I think of Aunt Polly, I recall first that final glimpse of her in the coffin, and it is only after an effort that I remember what a kind and generous soul she really was. In death, her face had none of its friendly glow, but looked stern and terrible. I took one frightened look and then hurried back to the kitchen.

There was little to reassure me there. The argument had been resumed, and my three uncles were glaring at one another. They stopped talking as soon as they saw me, but not before I had heard Uncle Arthur exclaim, in a voice utterly unlike his usual soft drawl, that the corner cupboard had been in this house for forty years and that he was damned if anybody was going to take it away now.

Soon Grandmother and Aunt Jennie came out of the bedroom, their eyes red with weeping. Aunt Jennie must have noticed how hunched up and frightened I looked, for she said: "Why don't you go out and look for Ben and Rose, Danny? They're playing around somewhere."

Glad to escape, I quickly put on my coat and ran outside. Before long I found my cousins, and we started a game of tag. For a little while it was fun, but then I remembered how strange Aunt Polly had looked in her coffin and a cold shiver ran through me. Ben and Rose didn't seem to have their hearts in the game either, and by mutual consent we gave it up and stood about awkwardly, shifting from foot to foot and wondering what to say.

"When are you coming out to the farm again, Dan?" asked Ben.

"I don't know. In the Christmas holidays, maybe."

A long pause, and then Rose said: "We have a lot more pigeons now."

"Are there any baby ones?" I asked, since some comment seemed called for.

"Baby ones — in November?" There was a slight curl on her lips as she said it, and for the first time I was aware of the farm child's scorn for the ignorance of the town-bred. I retreated into a shell of silence.

Ben picked up a stone and threw it at a tree. We all watched the curve of its flight. "Missed!" he said. He threw another stone, and it hit the trunk squarely. "I'll bet you can't hit it in three tries," he said to me.

I ignored the challenge. "Scared, eh?" he said. Then he looked at me sharply and asked: "Did you see her, in the coffin?"

"Yes."

"Were you scared?"

Fearing more ridicule, I lied. "No."

"I'll bet you were, though."

At that moment we heard Aunt Jennie calling us. It was time to get ready for the funeral.

Somehow I got through the funeral, hanging on tightly to Grandmother's hand. The worst part was when they lowered the coffin into the grave — I couldn't help seeing Aunt Polly inside it.

Afterwards we went back to Aunt Polly's house for supper. Everybody seemed relieved that the funeral was over, but didn't like to show it. Little was said. You could tell, though, from the furtive looks of my uncles, that they were waiting to renew their argument after Grandmother and I had gone home. It amazed me to see what appetites they all had, for I could eat nothing.

Grandmother and I had to leave just after supper to catch the last bus. Uncle Arthur walked to the station with us, and all the way he was telling Grandmother that he wouldn't have believed his two brothers could be so selfish. He had looked after his mother for twenty years, given her all his pay every week except a bit of pocket-money for himself, while they had never so much as lifted a finger for her. Of all the damned cheek, wanting to take the corner cupboard and the grandfather clock to them daft wives of theirs in Mansfield. He'd see them hanged first!

When I got to bed that night I couldn't sleep. I kept seeing that coffin and coming out in a sweat all over. Finally I gave up trying and sought comfort with Grandmother.

It was my first acquaintance with death, and I learned then that there is comfort only in the living and that even over the living death can cast an evil spell.

The Ghost of Reddleman Lane

I heard of the ghost of Reddleman Lane before I even reached the village of Girton. But I didn't expect that I should ever see it.

I had gone to England for the summer to visit my grandmother. As I was only twelve at the time, my mother was with me. We were riding in an ancient taxi which was taking us from the station in Collingham to the village where Grandmother lived. It was dark, the rain was beating against the windows of the car, and I was feeling pleasantly drowsy. Suddenly the taxi driver turned his huge red face towards us and said, "Keep your eyes peeled, son. This is Reddleman Lane."

"Reddleman Lane?" I asked, peering through the misty window beside me and seeing nothing but the vague outline of some tall bushes. "Why should I keep my eyes peeled?"

"For the Ghost, of course," the man said, cackling out of his brownstained teeth.

Mother took a hand. I could tell by the way she leaned forward and emphasized her words with sharp gestures of her hands that she was really angry. "Keep quiet, man. Do you want to scare the boy to death?"

"Oh, Mother, don't be silly," I said, my pride wounded. "You don't suppose I believe in ghosts, do you? It's just a silly old superstition. What *is* the story, driver?"

But the taximan had been offended by my mother's sharp rebuke, and he wouldn't say anything more. He just glared at the narrow gravel road ahead of him, his moutache jerking up and down as if he were resisting an impulse to spit. He reminded me of the pictures of the giant in *Jack and the Beanstalk*.

Anyway, his sudden outburst had wakened me up, and when we reached Grandmother's cottage in a few minutes I was full of questions. "Why do they call it Reddleman Lane? What is a 'reddleman'? Why is there supposed to be a ghost? When does the ghost walk?" But to all these and similar questions my mother refused to listen. She kept telling me to keep quiet so that she could talk to Grandmother. Eventually, after we had had bacon and eggs and some tea, I was sent off to bed.

The room I slept in was small, with a sloping ceiling on two sides. It should have seemed very cosy, but tonight, perhaps because it was strange, it made me feel uneasy and trapped. When I opened my eyes, it seemed as if the two sloping sides were closing in on me, about to snuff me out like a candle. When I closed my eyes, I could see the huge leering face of the taxi-driver — or was it of the Giant? — pressing closer and closer to my own.

Well, this was a pretty bad start for a boy who had always prided himself on his courage and commonsense. Just a bare reference to one of the ghosts which I had always heard were supposed to inhabit old English villages, and I was as nervous as a nine-year-old girl in a nightshirt! Come to your senses, I told myself. You know all these yarns about ghosts are just bait for American tourists.

I forced myself to get out of bed and go over to the tiny window — not much more than a foot square — which opened out of the right-hand wall of the room. But there was little to comfort me in the view outside. The rain was still pelting down, rushing in a regular torrent down the rainpipe beside my window, and sluicing into a big rainbarrel on the ground about twelve feet below. The moon had risen now, and in its fitful light — it kept being hidden by the clouds which were scudding across the sky like leaves in a gale — I could see my grandmother's garden and orchard. The branches of the trees were writhing and twisting in the wind and their leaves were whistling and hissing like startled geese. I went back to bed, covered my head with the blanket, and after a long time feel asleep.

I soon found plenty to do around Girton. Grandmother had an old bike one of my uncles had left there years before, and on it I explored the surrounding countryside. One of the first places I sought out was Reddleman Lane. Certainly in the daytime it didn't look particularly fearsome. It was only about a hundred yards long, and it ran from the main highway (part of the Old North Road, I discovered) to a branch road which skirted the river Fleet for a mile or so before entering the village of Girton. The only forbidding features of the lane were the extremely high hawthorn hedges which lined both its sides, and which made the roadway dark even at noon. I searched about in the hedge for some lingering traces of the gallows, but found nothing except some old tin cans and the occasional thrush's nest.

Yes, by this time I knew enough to look for the gallows. Although both Mother and Grandmother had refused to tell me anything about the ghost of Reddleman Lane, I had pieced the story together from fragments of information dropped by various villagers.

Reddleman Lane got its name from the fact that a reddleman had been hanged there one hundred and fifty years ago. A reddleman's job — extinct now for almost a hundred years — was to go around the country selling redding to farmers for marking their sheep. This particular reddleman had been accused and found guilty of stealing sheep, and had been hanged on a gallows set up in this lane. Ever since, so the story went, his ghost had walked every midnight.

The story haunted me, though my reason told me that it was merely idle gossip. In the daytime, riding my bicycle around the country roads, learning to play cricket in the meadow by the Fleet with the village boys, or fishing in the river and its tributary streams, I was so occupied that I paid little attention to the ghostly legend. But at night-time, trying to get to sleep in the tiny room beneath the sloping ceilings, I could think of nothing else but the dark, mysterious lane and its grisly occupant.

I began to feel that the only way for me to rid myself of this obsession was to visit the lane at midnight. Finding nothing, as I was convinced I should, I should be able to relax and discuss the tale. Many times I went to the small window of my bedroom, trying to gather my courage to make the eerie pilgrimage. At last, one night when the moon was high and full and my grandmother's garden almost as bright as day, I began the great experiment.

By opening the window to its fullest extent, I managed to squeeze through it. Then I shinnied down the rainpipe, rested my feet on the edge of the softwater barrel, and jumped to the ground.

Quickly I opened the coalshed, got out my bicycle, and headed along the village street towards the Fleet.

Although it was not quite midnight, every light in the village had long been put out — these people, mainly farmers and farm labourers, went to bed early. Once, as I passed a garden gate, a dog barked violently and made me jump so badly that I almost fell off my bike. As I reached the road by the river, I could see the still water of the Fleet glimmering in the moonlight, looping through the low-lying meadows like a carelessly thrown silver shawl.

As I approached the dark tunnel of Reddleman Lane my heart began to thump and my hands grew moist with sweat. Jumping off my bike and throwing it down in the grass beside the road, I looked at my watch in the moonlight. It was five minutes to twelve.

Trying for some reason which I can't really explain to make as little noise as possible, I gingerly tiptoed down the lane, and took up a position in the shadow of the high hedge. For a minute or two there was neither sound nor motion. Then my straining ears seemed to catch a faint, distant rumble, as of a cart passing over gravel. I peered towards the Fleet Road, but could see nothing except the stretch of meadow grass and the far glimmer of the water.

Now I could make out a vague, dark, roughly rectangular shape moving along the Fleet Road towards the entrance of the lane. The sound now was more distinct: I could make out the dull clop-clop of a horse's hooves, and the half-rumbling, half grinding noise of wheels turning on gravel.

Yes, it was a wagon, an old fashioned affair similar to the covered wagons used by the American pioneers. But it differed from them in colour. Every inch of it, except the steel rims of the wheels which flashed in the moonlight like scimitars, was lurid red. It was pulled slowly forward by an old grey horse, whose hide was generously flecked with red patches that looked like raw wounds.

This was disconcerting enough; but beside the wagon walked a human figure even more strange. From the tip of the cap to the heel of his boots he was blood red! Even his face and his hands were red. In the vivid light of the full moon he glowed like a fiery gem.

Now the wagon and its strange conductor had entered the darkness of the lane, and the bright red of their colouring dulled to a mere blur. They were getting closer and closer to me, and my impulse was to run. What held me to my place was the knowledge that my bike lay behind them, and to get to it was my best hope of escape. Perhaps if I stayed quiet in the bushes, the ghostly visitant would pass me by unnoticed.

The wagon was almost opposite my hiding place now. Even in the dim light of the lane its red sides glowed like the embers of a coal fire. The reddleman kept his eyes straight ahead on the road, and the grey horse plodded steadily forward. He was going to pass me by!

But at the very last moment the horse, as if by his own volition, stopped in front of me. The reddleman turned his head and looked at me. I had expected to see an old man, but his red face was smooth and young. His clothes — a tight-fitting suit of some material like corduroy — were as red as his face. Only his lips and his eyes were exceptions to the prevailing red. His lips looked almost white, and his eyes were light blue. He kept his eyes upon me for a full minute, and they seemed to burn their way into my very soul. I braced myself for a torrent of curses, but he said nothing.

Suddenly he moved towards me and put out his hand. For a moment his hand gripped my sleeve, and I felt his vice-like fingers tighten upon the flesh of my arm. At first I was paralyzed with fear; then, as his fierce red face came closer to my own, I ducked and twisted and somehow squirmed my way out of his grip. I rushed toward my bike, jumped on, and pedalled furiously down the lane towards the Fleet Road.

I raced home to the village without even pausing to look back. My tires crunched and bounced over the pebbles, but I kept the pedals turning as swiftly as if I were racing on a smooth indoor track. I looked neither at the river beside me nor at the full moon in the sky above, but kept my eyes firmly on the road ahead.

At last I reached my grandmother's house. Without pausing to put my bike in its shed, I threw the machine against the wall of the house, jumped on the rainbarrel, shinnied up the rainpipe, and clambered through the window into my room.

As I put out my right arm to close the window after me, I saw for the first time something which chilled my spine. On the sleeve of my jacket, sharply outlined in vivid red, was the print of a large hand!

The Lost Girl

It was a bright, hot Sunday in early August, and the crowds had come to this beach from all over the island. Three big buses had brought a contingent of sea-cadets and their band. Sleek new cars had swished in from the cities and towns, and old battered trucks had rattled in from remote villages and farms. Their occupants had poured out to join the tourists who were spending a week or a month in the tents, trailers, cabins, and hotels which clustered around the beach.

There were people everywhere. Even the paths along the top of the red sandstone cliffs, almost deserted on week days, were crowded with picnickers, camera fans, and romping children. But the crowd was thickest in two places — on the flat, open, grassy area which lay behind the sand-dunes, and on the beach itself, which stretched for several miles between the dunes and the sea.

Behind the dunes were the buildings and other facilities provided by the National Parks Service. Here was the canteen, its platform jammed with sailors and shop girls who bought hot dogs and pop with such speed that the children who swarmed between their legs hoping to buy gum or chocolate bars were almost ignored. Here too was the recreation hall: on week-nights it was the scene of National Film Board movies or square dances called to the twang of an old piano, but this afternoon its chairs were occupied by elderly farm-women who were bent on having somehow the good lazy gossip they would have preferred to have on their own shady verandas.

On a patch of lightly grassed sand near the trailer park were the sea-cadet band and their jostling listeners. Clad in their billowing navy-blue trousers and tight matching jumpers, white sailor-hats perched flatly on their heads, the cadets puffed and huffed at their brass instruments with such energy that it seemed their cheeks must burst or their eyes pop out of their sockets.

Nearby were the changing houses, around which teen-agers of both sexes in brief swimsuits chased each other in amorous play. On the horseshoe pitches, elderly farmers in shirt-sleeves and galluses took careful aim and threw their clanging shoes, while on the softball diamond young shoe-clerks and insurance salesman showed their circle of watching wives that they could still throw a mean curve or belt a long ball. At the very foot of the dunes was the children's playground, dotted with swings and slides and teeter-totters over which hordes of children squirmed and swarmed like ants.

On the beach on the other side of the dunes the crowds were even thicker. As far as the eye could see, and the beach extended for a good five miles, there were people and more people. The more elderly sat stiffly in the blue serge suits or pastel cotton dresses they had worn to church that morning; the young adults lay stretched on the sand in their swimsuits and soaked up the sunshine; the youths and children danced in and out of the water scattering spray in all directions, or dug furiously in the sand as they constructed moats, castles and underground tunnels.

So thickly were the people clustered that it was almost impossible to single out individuals — but there was one who caught the eye. An old man of about seventy, his badly misshapen back set him apart from the crowd. An old farmer by the look of him, he wore a shabby blue suit with faint red stripes and a faded yellow straw hat. He had pulled the hat down over his forehead to shade his eyes from the sun, and he sat facing the sea with his hands stretched out behind him on the sand. In a group with him were half a dozen men and women slightly younger than himself. From time to time members of the group exchanged comments on the weather, the crowds, individuals, or the children.

"Best Sunday of the summer."

"You can say that again."

"Couldn't be better."

"Never seen so many here."

"No, but just wait till they build that causeway."

"Won't seem like the Island then."

"See that woman! Does she think that outfit is decent?"

"Well, if you've got it you may as well show it!"

"Now, George, watch what you're saying!"

"Look at those kids! Having the time of their lives aren't they?"

"Wish I had half their energy!"

"Isn't that little girl the cutest thing?"

But the old man said very little. He was watching the children.

There were four children playing in the water directly in front of him, and he watched them almost constantly. There were two boys of about twelve and ten, and two girls of about eight and six. They seemed to be brothers and sisters, and they all had black hair and pale faces, thin bony arms and legs, and wore faded bathing suits that had obviously been handed down through the seasons.

Those whom the old man took to be the parents of the children, sat together a little way down the beach. The mother, looking even more unhealthy than the children, had a thin, pinched pale face, a perpetually worried and fretful expression, and clutched a tiny, restless infant to her light blue cotton dress. The father was tall, thin and ungainly, and he stared out to sea with an expression of bored irritation.

But there was nothing bored about the children. They raced into the water, swam a few awkward but thrilling strokes with breath tightly held, splashed each other, ran ahead of the incoming surf up the beach, then turned back and jumped into the sea. When they grew tired of running and spashing, they sat in the sand and scooped together houses and castles with their hands. Occasionally they had a brief quarrel among themselves. When this happened, their mother called angrily to them to stop, and their father glared at them; but they seemed to pay little attention and soon made up the quarrel among themselves.

The old man watched their every move. The youngest girl, the little creature of six, seemed especially to fascinate him. She was the most delicate looking of the four: so thin was she that it seemed her skin was simply stretched over her bones. And yet she was tremendously alive: her dark brown eyes glittered with joy, and her legs and arms were always in motion.

The afternoon gradually ran down like a clock that no one had rewound. The sun was still shining, but it had lost its power, and the sea air had now a faint warning chill. The paths along the top of the cliffs were littered with the leavings of departed picnickers; only here and there were a few strollers trying to get one last snapshot before the light failed. There were a good many gaps in the parking lot, and the air was filled with the whirr of starters and the loud purr of freshly choked motors. Hot dogs and hamburgers were still being sold at the canteen, but the appetites of buyers were less keen and the few children had no difficulty in pressing their sticky nickels into the hands of the tired salesmen.

A few hangers-on still exchanged gossip in the recreation hall, but there were long bored silences and frequent glances at the clock which hung on the wall beside the stage. A faint mutter of voices came from the changing houses, but the teen-agers were no longer chasing and admiring each other. The band had stopped playing an hour ago, the instruments had been stowed away in their cases and packed into the luggage compartment of the bus, and now the blown-out bandsmen were piling into the seats ready for the long, noisy ride home. The softball diamond was deserted, and the horseshoe pitchers had gone home.

At the children's playground a few impatient parents gave Johnny or Susie their last turn.

"Now look here, Johnny, it's past time we'd gone home!"

"Haven't you had enough slides for one day?"

"All right, then. One more swing. And this is the last remember."

"Oh come on, for goodness sake!"

"Susie, get off that slide!"

On the beach there were still a few late picnickers, watching the sun set slowly at the far edge of the sea and touch all the waves with gold. The four children and their parents had disappeared over the dunes half an hour ago, but the old man and his companions still lingered.

The old man sighed, stood up, and brushed the sand from his trousers.

"Well," he said, "the children have gone, the sun's going, and I guess we may as well go home."

His companions stood up too, gathered up their lunch-basket and other belongings, shook the sand out of their blanket, and walked slowly with the old man through the sand.

Up the green slatted boardwalk they climbed, the old man with crooked back in the lead. At the crest of the dune he stopped, turned and looked out to sea.

"The end of a perfect day," he said. "Just look at that sunset."

As he turned back towards the land he suddenly became aware of something wrong. It was nothing definite at first, just a faint stir of anxiety, a quick sense of disquiet. He looked down towards the children's playground and saw that a small crowd was gathering at the end of the boardwalk. He hobbled down the slats toward them, struck by their anxious faces.

Then he heard a wail, a sob, a long drawn out cry of anguish. It pierced him like a blade. He could not see her yet, but instinctively he knew from whom the wail came.

"Good God!" he said. "It's the little girl!"

Now he saw her, the six-year-old, hysterical, running in short futile circles this way and that. She stamped her foot, made a pathetic leap into the air, pulled desperately at her hair. Never had he seen such embodied misery, such terror. The girl had become all the fear and desolation of the world jammed into one small exploding packet of flesh. Her helpless anguish gripped and twisted his heart until it seemed that it too must burst.

"Mummy, oh Mummy! Mu-u-u-u-mmy!"

The child waited, sobbed, stamped her foot, ran a few steps away from the crowd, returned, shook her hand forlornly at the darkening sky.

Her anguish was reflected in every face around her. They stared at her helplessly, they looked at one another, they stared back at her. Most of them stood as if paralyzed. One or two of the women tried to touch her, but she would not let them come near her.

A middle-aged matron with straight grey hair stepped towards the girl and asked her a series of questions — "What does your mother look like? Where did she leave you? Where did you see her last? Where do you live? What colour dress is your mother wearing?" — but the girl was too terrified to answer. She ran more and more frantically back and forth, twisting and plunging like a rabbit trapped in the last thin strand of grain.

More and more people were collecting — everybody who was left near the beach seemed to have heard the girl's screams now and to have been drawn here by a wrenching pity. But nobody knew what to do.

"We should take her to the recreation hall. That's where her mother would look for her."

"Fancy leaving a little tot like that alone!"

"Where do you suppose her mother is? Drunk some place, probably."

"My God, I can't take it! That screaming!"

"Can't anyone do anything for her?"

"We'd be glad to take her home with us."

"I'd drive her anywhere, if she'd only say where her home is."

"We can't leave her here."

"If only we could stop her crying."

The old man felt the general pity, the general helplessness. What could he do? Would she let him help her, touch her, ask her, when she wouldn't let the others? His crooked back might scare her.

Yes, her name. If only he could remember her name, he might be able to soothe her. What had he heard her brothers and sisters calling her? Marjorie — no, he had it now, Margy.

"Margy!" he called, forcing his voice to sound natural.

She stopped leaping about, looked about the crowd for the source of her name. He stepped forward. "Remember me, Margy?"

he said. She didn't run away, but stood quietly watching him. "Remember, I sat near you on the beach all afternoon. I'd know your mother if I saw her."

She let him go up to her, let him rest his hand lightly on her shoulder. She was still sobbing, but in the dry, choking gasps that are the aftermath of grief.

He had another inspiration. He put his hand in his pocket and fished out a nickel. "Here's a nickel," he said. Shall we go and get an icecream cone at the canteen? Maybe we'll find your mother over there."

It worked. She held out her hand and took the nickel, then gave him her other hand to hold. Together they began to walk towards the canteen. The people in the crowd sighed with relief, some followed the old man and the girl, others headed for their cars.

"Fancy that! The old man knew how to handle her."

"I hope he finds her mother soon."

"I wonder how long he'll be able to keep her quiet?"

"Oh, she'll be all right now."

The old man and the girl were just stepping on to the road that separated the playground from the canteen when a car drew up and stopped.

"It's Mummy!" cried the girl. She darted away from the old man and grabbed at the car door.

The door was opened from the inside and the girl's mother stepped out. She pushed the girl roughly into the car.

"Margy, you bad girl," said her mother. "What was the big idea? Disappearing like that! Didn't I tell you to wait right by the canteen?" She crowded back into the car, pushing the girl before her.

The old man reached over the woman and dropped a quarter into the little girl's hand. "There you are, Margy. Buy yourself something nice tomorrow." Then, addressing the mother, he said, "Don't be hard on her, missus. The poor kid was nearly scared out of her wits."

The mother turned on him. "Here, what's going on anyway? Whose business are you sticking your nose into? And where were you planning to take her anyway, you dirty old man?"

"Oh, Mummy," said the little girl. "He's nice. He was going to buy me an icecream cone."

"I've heard that tale before!" said the mother.

"Oh, cut the cackle, you two," said the child's father. "Let's get going. We're an hour late now." He let the clutch in with a jerk, and the car snorted up the road.

The old man watched it out of sight, then he turned wearily back to look for his relatives.

The sun had set now, and the dusk was rapidly gathering over the cliffs, the softball diamond, the horse-shoe pitch, the playground, and the dunes. They were putting up the shutters at the canteen, the recreation hall was dark and silent, and the swings hung empty in the cool evening air. From beyond the dunes came the faint murmur of the cold and restless sea.

Bibliography

WORKS BY DESMOND PACEY

I. — SHORT STORIES

"Parade," *Farmer's Magazine*, November, 1938, pp. 30-31.

"Homecoming," *Acta Victoriana*, LXI (January, 1937), 4-5.

"And the Gods Laughed," *Acta Victoriana*, LXII (April, 1938), 1-4.

"Hired Man," *Queen's Quarterly*, XLVIII (1941), 268-276.

"Aunt Polly," *Queen's Quarterly*, LIII (1946), 209-217.

"Silo," *Family Herald and Weekly Star*, LXXVII (1947), 18-19.

"The Field of Oats," *Hilltop*, I, no. 1 (April, 1948), 12-18.

"No Young Man," *Canadian Forum*, XXIX (1949), 38-39.

"The Good Hope," *Queen's Quarterly*, LVII (1950), 209-217.
— Reprinted as "The Boat," in *The Picnic and Other Stories*, Toronto: Ryerson, 1958, pp. 10-19. Also published under that title in *Neue Illustrierte* and in *National Zeitung* (Basel). Also published in *Du* (Zurich) and in *Fordrevue* (Munich), *Arbeiter Zeitung, Der gute Kamerad, Aachener Kirchenzeitung, Hannov. Presse, Berner Tageblatt*, 1971.

"The Picnic," *Northern Review*, IV (1950), 36-41.
— Also published in German in *Neue Illustrierte*, June 23, 1956, and in *National Zeitung*, Basel, Sept. 9, 1956, and in *Du*, October, 1956, and in *Rhein-Neckar-Zeitung*, 1971.

"The Mirror," *Dalhousie Review*, XXXIX (1954), 155-159.

"That Day in the Bush," *Canadian Forum*, XXXIV (1955), 226-227.

"Memoirs of a Hitchhiker," *Atlantic Advocate*, XLVII (December, 1956), 66-68.

"The Ghost of Reddleman Lane," *Atlantic Advocate*, XLVII (December, 1957), 45, 47-48.
— (Reprinted), *Beckoning Trails*, ed. P. W. Diebel and Madeline Young, Toronto: Ryerson, 1962.

"The Odour of Incense," *Canadian Forum*, XXXVII (1957), 42-44.
— (Reprinted), *Stories with John Drainie*, ed. John Drainie, Toronto: Ryerson Press, 1963, pp. 198-206.

"The Lost Girl," *Atlantic Advocate,* XLIX (January, 1958), 79-82.

— (Reprinted), *Atlantic Anthology,* ed. Will R. Bird, Toronto: McClelland & Stewart, 1959, pp. 236-242.

"The Misses York," broadcast in "Canadian Short Stories" series by C.B.C. and printed in *The Picnic and Other Stories,* Toronto: Ryerson, 1958.

"The Test," printed in *The Picnic and Other Stories* (1958).

"A Moment of Love," *Atlantic Advocate,* XLVIII (April, 1958), 80-81.

"The Visit," *Atlantic Advocate,* L (February, 1960), 82-85.

— Reprinted as "The Trespasser," in *The Picnic and Other Stories* (1958).

"The Weasel," *Canadian Forum,* XXXIX (1960), 260-261.

"The Brothers," *Atlantic Advocate,* LI (May, 1961), 69-73.

"When She Comes Over," *The Fiddlehead,* no. 53 (Summer, 1962), 21-26.

"The Candidate," *Atlantic Advocate,* LIII (March, 1963), 78-83.

"The Life and Death of Morning Star," *Atlantic Advocate,* LIV (April, 1964), 33-38.

"A Fellow of Christhouse," *Atlantic Advocate,* LVII (September, 1966), 65-72.

"First Date," *Atlantic Advocate,* LVIII (June, 1968), 69-73.

"On the Roman Road," *Atlantic Advocate,* LX (May, 1970), 35-57.

"Waken Lords and Ladies Gay", *Atlantic Advocate,* 62 (April, 1972), 18-20, 22.

"A Summer Afternoon," *Atlantic Advocate,* Vol. 62, No. 12 (August, 1972), pp. 28-31.

II. — POEMS

"Prairie Episode," *The Fiddlehead,* no. 1 (February, 1945).

"The Flavour of Now," *The Fiddlehead,* no. 2 (April, 1945).

"Revised Version," *The Fiddlehead,* no. 3 (October, 1945).

"Monument," *The Fiddlehead,* no. 3 (October, 1945).

"Lines to a Politician," *The Fiddlehead,* no. 4 (February, 1946).

"No Sedative can Soothe the Heart," *The Fiddlehead,* no. 5 (November, 1946).

"Vignettes of Love," *The Fiddlehead,* no. 6 (February, 1947).

"The Prairie," *The Fiddlehead,* no. 7 (December, 1947).

III. — OTHER WRITINGS
A. Books

Frederick Philip Grove, a biographical and critical study. Toronto: Ryerson, 1945.

The Cow With the Musical Moo, and Other Verses for Children, illustrated by Milada Horejs and Karel Rohlicek. Fredericton, N.B.: Brunswick Press, 1952. iv, unpaged, col. illus.

Hippity Hobo and the Bee, and Other Verses for Children, illustrated by Milada Horejs and Karel Rohlicek. Fredericton, N.B.: Brunswick Press, 1952. iv, unpaged, col. illus.

Creative Writing in Canada, a Short History of English-Canadian Literature, Toronto: Ryerson Press, 1952.
— Second edition. Revised and enlarged, 1961.
— Paperback edition, 1966.

The Picnic and Other Stories, with a foreword by Roy Daniells. Toronto: Ryerson, 1958.

Ten Canadian Poets, a Group of Biographical and Critical Essays, Toronto: Ryerson: 1958.
— 1st paperback edition. 1966.

The Cat, The Cow, and The Kangaroo. The Collected Children's Verse of Desmond Pacey. Illustrated by Mary Pacey. Fredericton, N.B.: Brunswick Press, 1967.

Ethel Wilson, Twayne Publishers, New York: 1968.

Essays in Canadian Criticism, Ryerson, Toronto: 1969.

B. Editor of:

A Book of Canadian Stories, Toronto: Ryerson, 1947.
— 2nd edition, rev. and enl. Toronto: Ryerson, 1950.
— (School ed.) Toronto: Ryerson, 1952.
— 3rd edition, rev. and enl. Toronto: Ryerson, 1961.
— Toronto: Ryerson Press, 1967, first paperback edition.

The Selected Poems of Sir Charles G. D. Roberts, 1860-1943. Edited with an introduction by Desmond Pacey. Toronto: Ryerson, 1956.

Delight, by Mazo de la Roche. Edited with an introduction by Desmond Pacey, New Canadian Library, Toronto: McClelland & Stewart, 1960.

Swamp Angel, by Ethel Wilson, ed. with an introduction by Desmond Pacey, New Canadian Library, Toronto: McClelland & Stewart, 1962.

The Literary Review, VIII (Summer, 1965). 433-576 pp. (Special Canadian Number). Guest Editor.

Our Literary Heritage, an anthology of literature in English, Toronto: Ryerson Press and Macmillan, 1966.

The Harbour Master, by Theodore G. Roberts, edited with an introduction by Desmond Pacey, New Canadian Library, Toronto: McClelland & Stewart, 1968.

Frederick Philip Grove, "Critical Views of Canadian Writers", Toronto: Ryerson Press, 1970.

Tales from the Margin, the Selected Short Stories of Frederick Philip Grove, Toronto: Ryerson Press, 1971.

C. Co-editor of:

New Voices. Canadian University Writing of 1956, selected by Earle Birney and others, foreword by Joseph McCulley, Toronto: Dent, 1956.

Literary History of Canada. Ed. Carl F. Klinck, et al., Toronto: University of Toronto Press, 1965.

D. Sections of books:

"Introduction," *The Selected Poems of Dorothy Livesay,* Toronto: Ryerson, 1957, pp. xi-xix.

"The Canadian Writer and His Public, 1881-1952," *Studia Varia,* I (1957), 11-20.

"Sir Charles G. D. Roberts," *Our Living Tradition, Fourth Series,* Ed. Robert L. McDougall, Toronto: University of Toronto Press, 1962, pp. 31-56.

"The Threat of Nuclear Warfare," *This is My Concern,* ed. Foster M. Russell, Coburg: Northumberland Book Co., 1962, pp. 75-77.

"Fiction (1920-1940)," *Literary History of Canada: Canadian Literature in English,* ed. Carl F. Klinck, Toronto: University of Toronto Press, 1965, pp. 658-693.

"The Writer and His Public," *Literary History of Canada: Canadian Literature in English,* ed. Carl F. Klinck et al., Toronto: University of Toronto Press, 1965, pp. 477-495.

"Contemporary Writing in New Brunswick," *The Arts in New Brunswick,* ed. R. A. Tweedie et al., Fredericton: Brunswick Press, 1967, pp. 33-40.

"English-Canadian Poets, 1944-1954," *The Making of Modern Poetry in Canada,* ed. Louis Dudek and Michael Gnarowski, Toronto: Ryerson Press, 1967, pp. 160-169.

"My Thoughts on Americans and the U.S.A.," *The New Romans*, Edmonton: Hurlig, 1968, pp. 156-158.

"L'Écrivain et son public 1929-1960", "Le Roman 1920-1940", *Histoire littéraire du Canada*, ed. C. F. Klinck et al, traduit de l'anglais par M. Lebel, Québec: Les Presses de l'Université Laval, 1970, pp. 573-594, 784-825.

"A Reading of Lampman's 'Heat'," *Critical Views on Canadian Writers: Archibald Lampman*, ed. M. Gnarowski, Toronto: Ryerson, 1970, 178-184.

"Earthy Idyll," *Critical Views on Canadian Writers, Ernest Buckler*, by Gregory M. Cook, Toronto: McGraw-Hill Ryerson Limited, 1972, pp. 127-8.

Essays on Hugh Garner, Norman Levine, Brian Moore, Sinclair Ross, Ethel Wilson, in *Contemporary Novelists*, Ed. James Vinson, New York: St. Martin's Press, 1972, pp. 452, 761, 899, 1070, 1385.

IV. — ARTICLES

"Centenary Celebration," *Acta Victoriana*, LX (April, 1936), 28.

"In Search of Apron Strings," *Acta Victoriana*, XLI (October, 1936), 3-5.

"Look Homeward, Angel," *Acta Victoriana*, XLI (December, 1936), 15-17.

"The Modern Novel," *Acta Victoriana*, XLI (February, 1937), 31-33.

"Prolegomenon," *Acta Victoriana*, XLI (March, 1937), 17-18.

"The Modern Novel," *Acta Victoriana*, XLI (March, 1937), 31-33.

"Tradition Upheld," *Acta Victoriana*, LXII (November, 1937), 17-19.

"Pity the Writer!" *Acta Victoriana*, LXII (December, 1937), 10-12.

"Letter, Lecture and Lethargy," *Acta Victoriana*, LXII (January, 1938), 19-21.

"The March of Time," *Acta Victoriana*, LXII (February, 1938), 18-21.

"Prospect and Retrospect," *Acta Victoriana*, LXII (April, 1938), 15-18.

"At last — A Canadian Literature?" *Cambridge Review*, LX (December, 1938), 146-147.

"Balzac and Thackeray," *Modern Language Review*, XXXVI (1941), 213-224.

"Henry James and His French Contemporaries," *American Literature*, XIII (1941), 239-256.

"Frederick Philip Grove," *Manitoba Arts Review*, III (1943), 28-41.

"The Humanities in Canada," *Queen's Quarterly*, L (1943-1944), 354-360.

"In Defence of Basic English..." *Queen's Quarterly*, LI (1944), 117-123.

"The Future of Universities: a British View," *Queen's Quarterly*, LI (1944), 420-428.

"The Novel in Canada," *Queen's Quarterly*, LII (1945), 322-331.

"A Probable Addition to the Thackeray Canon," *Publications of the Modern Language Association of America*, LX (1945), 607-611.

"Washington Irving and Charles Dickens," *American Literature*, XVI, 1945, 331-339.

"The First Canadian Novel," *Dalhousie Review*, XXVI (1946), 143-150.

"Flaubert and His Victorian Critics....," *University of Toronto Quarterly*, XVI (1946), 78-84.

"In Defense of Liberalism," *Canadian Forum*, XXV (1946), 238-239.

"The State of Canadian Poetry," *Canadian Student*, XXIV (1946), 53-54, 59.

"The Future of the Novel" *Queen's Quarterly*, LIV (1947), 74-93.

"The Poetry of Duncan Campbell Scott," *Canadian Forum*, XXVIII (1948), 107-109.

"Virginia Woolf as a Literary Critic," *University of Toronto Quarterly*, XVII (1948), 234-244.

"How Big Should Our Universities Be?" *Dalhousie Review*, XXIX (1949), 146-152.

"Bliss Carman: A Reappraisal," *Northern Review*, III (Feb.-Mar., 1950), 2-10.

"Literary Criticism in Canada," *University of Toronto Quarterly*, XIX (1950), 113-119.

"The Goldsmiths and Their Villages," *University of Toronto Quarterly*, XXI (1951), 27-38.

"Service and MacInnes," *Northern Review*, IV (Feb.-Mar., 1951), 12-17.

"Some Recent English Canadian Novels," *La Nouvelle Revue Canadienne*, I (novembre-décembre, 1951), 52-55.

"Leacock as a Satirist," *Queen's Quarterly*, LVIII (1951), 208-219.

"Two Accents, One Voice," *Saturday Review of Literature*, XXXV (June 7, 1952), 15-16.

"Areas of Research in Canadian Literature," *University of Toronto Quarterly*, XXIII (October, 1953), 58-63.

"A Reading of Lampman's 'Heat'," *Culture*, XIV (1953), 292-297.

"English-Canadian Poetry, 1944-1954," *Culture*, XV (1954), 255-265.

"The Innocent Eye: the Art of Ethel Wilson," *Queen's Quarterly*, LXI (1954), 42-52.

BIBLIOGRAPHY

"The Role of the Critic," *Canadian Author and Bookman,* XXXII (Summer, 1956), 24-26.

"A Group of Seven," *Queen's Quarterly,* LXIII (Autumn, 1956), 436-443.

"A Colonial Romantic: Major John Richardson, Soldier and Novelist," *Canadian Literature,* number 2 (1959), 20-31; number 3 (1960), 47-56.

"Bruno Bobak at U.N.B.," *Canadian Art,* XVIII (March-April, 1961), 140-142.

"A Garland for Bliss Carman," *Atlantic Advocate,* LI (April, 1961), 17, 19-20, 23-24.

"The Young Writer and the Canadian Cultural Milieu," *Queen's Quarterly,* LXIX (1962), 378-390.

"What the University Expects," *Vital English,* I (June, 1964), 7-9.

"Cambridge Revisited," *Atlantic Advocate,* LIV (May, 1964), 46-51.

"A Visit to Hardy's Wessex," *Atlantic Advocate,* LV (November, 1964), 54-59.

"The Canadian Imagination," *The Literary Review,* VIII (Summer, 1965), 437-444.

"Easter Homage to George Herbert," *Atlantic Advocate,* LV (April, 1965), 40-44.

"A Night North of Rome," *Atlantic Advocate,* LV (June, 1965), 46-49.

"Lost in Aix-en-Provence," *Atlantic Advocate,* LV (February, 1965), 55-58.

"An Afternoon with Henry Moore," *Atlantic Advocate,* LV (July, 1965), 67-72.

"Ethel Wilson's First Novel," *Canadian Literature,* XXIX (Summer, 1966), 43-55.

"Canadian Literature, 1966," *Commentator,* XI (Jan., 1967), 22-25.

"On Becoming a Canadian," *Atlantic Advocate,* LVII (February, 1967), 12-13, 15.

"The Phenomenon of Leonard Cohen," *Canadian Literature,* No. 34, (Autumn, 1967), 5-23.

"The Outlook for Canadian Literature," *Canadian Literature,* No. 36, (Spring, 1968), 15-25.

"A Note on Major John Richardson," *Canadian Literature,* 39 (Winter, 1969), 103-4.

"A Plea for the Study of Our Own Literature," *Manitoba Curriculum Bulletin,* III (May, 1969), 3-4.

"The Return of a Native; Impressions of New Zealand," *Atlantic Advocate,* LIX (August, 1969), 31-35.

"A Canadian Quintet," *The Fiddlehead,* 83 (Jan.-Feb. 1970), 79-86.

"Church Life in Canada a Century Ago," *Atlantic Advocate,* LX (March, 1970), 45-52.

"Children in the Poetry of Yeats," *Dalhousie Review*, L (Summer, 1970), 233-248.

"Where will Norman Go Next?", *Atlantic Advocate*, (May, 1971), 59-63.

"In Search of Grove in Sweden: A Progress Report," *Journal of Canadian Fiction*, Vol. 1, No. 1, Winter 1972, 69-73.

V. — ENCYCLOPEDIA CONTRIBUTIONS

"Canada's Poets and Prose Writers," *The Book of Knowledge*, Grolier Society, 1948. (This article was rewritten for the 1956 ed.).

"Canadian Poets and Prose Writers," *The Book of Knowledge*, New York: Grolier, revised ed. 1956.

"Louise Morey Bowman," "W. A. Fraser," "Frederick Philip Grove," "John Hunter-Duvar," "Basil King," "A. M. Klein," "Mrs. Leprohon," "Tom MacInnes," "F. R. Scott," and "F. W. Wallace," *Encyclopedia Canadiana*, Ottawa: Canadiana Co. Ltd., 1956.

"Canadian Literature," "Frances Brooke," "L. J. Burpee," "Morley Callaghan," "J. C. Dent," "Roger Lemelin," "Hugh MacLennan," "W. Archibald MacMechan," "Charles Mair," "Gabrielle Roy," — all in *The World Book Encyclopedia* (1960).

"Canadian Literature," *American Educator Encyclopedia*. Lake Bluff, Ills., Tangley Oaks Education Centre, 1960.

"Fredericton, N.B." and "Frederick Philip Grove," "William Kirby," "Sir C. G. D. Roberts" — in *Encyclopedia Brittanica* (1961).

"Canadian Literature," in *Encyclopedia International*, (1967).

"Canadian Literature," in *Encyclopedia Americana*, (1967).

Biographies of Oliver Goldsmith, Thomas Chandler Haliburton, Charles Heavysege, Susanne Moodie and Mrs. Catherine Parr Traill in *The Encyclopedia of World Biography*, McGraw-Hill, New York, (1970).

Articles on "Canadian Literature" and "Pauline Johnson" in *The World Book Encyclopedia*.

VI. — PLAY

"Tea for Three," a play in one act. Directed by David Galloway and produced at the University of New Brunswick, August, 1952.

VII. — LETTERS

"The Issue," in *Acta Victoriana*, LX (November, 1935), 23.

"The Narrow Way," in *Times Literary Supplement*, no. 3364, 65th year, (Thursday, 18 August 1966), 743.

WORKS ABOUT DESMOND PACEY

Atlantic Advocate, IL (November 1958), 63.

BEATTIE, Munro, "Turning New Leaves", *The Canadian Forum,* XXXVIII (June 1958), 65-66.

BENNET, C. L., *"The Dalhousie Review,* XXXVIII, 2 (Summer 1958), 269, 271.

"Canadian Fiction", *Queen's Quarterly,* LV (Spring 1948), 112-13.

"Canadian Voices", *Saturday Night,* LXXIII (March 15, 1958), 39-40.

CHILD, Philip, *University of Toronto Quarterly,* XV (April 1946), 320-21.

CLARKE, George H., "A Canadian Novelist and His Critic", *Queen's Quarterly* (Autumn 1946), 362-68.

COGSWELL, Fred., *The Fiddlehead,* 28 (May 1956), 33, 35.

DANIELLS, Roy, "Landscape with Figures", *Canadian Literature,* 51 (Winter 1972).
— "Lorne Pierce Medal", *Royal Society of Canada Proceeding and Transactions,* X, 4th Ser., 1972, 26.

DEWAR, John A., "Canadian Novelist", *The Canadian Forum,* XXVI (November 1946), 186.

DOBBS, Kildare, "Miss Crotchett's Muse", *Tamarack Review,* 8 (Summer 1958), 87-92.

DUDEK, Louis, *The Canadian Forum,* XXXIX (May 1959), 45-46.

Echoes, March 1946, 40.

EDWARDS, Mary Jane, "Bird's-Eye View", *Canadian Literature,* 45 (Summer 1970), 93-95.

The Fiddlehead, XIX (November 1953), 11, 13.

FISHER, J., "Turning New Leaves", *The Canadian Forum,* XXVII (December 1947), 211.

GUNDY, H. P., "Canadian Literature", *Queen's Quarterly,* LIX (Autumn 1952), 404-05.

HANSON, W. A., *The Canadian Forum,* IL (March 1970), 295.

HENDERSON, T. G., "Humanities", *University of Toronto Quarterly,* XXXI (July 1962), 479-80.

KEITH, W. J., *University of Toronto Quarterly,* XLI (Summer 1972), 405-06.

KING, Carlyle, *The Canadian Forum,* XXXII (June 1952), 68.
— "Canadian", *Canadian Historical Review,* XXXIX, 4 (December 1958), 337-39.

KING, Carlyle, *University of Toronto Quarterly*, XXXVIII, (4 July 1969), 396-97.

KLINCK, Carl F., *The Fiddlehead*, 37 (Summer 1958), 41-44.

— *University of Toronto Quarterly*, XXXIX (July 1970), 373-74.

LAYTON, Irving, *The Fiddlehead*, 39 (Winter 1959), 41-43.

LAWRENCE, Robert G., *B.C. Library Quarterly*, XXXIII, 3 (January 1970), 15-16.

"Literary and Critical Studies", *University of Toronto Quarterly*, XXII (April 1953), 306-07.

"Littérature Canadienne d'Imagination", *Revue de l'Université Laval*, VII (October 1952), 185-87.

MANDEL, Eli., "Creative Writing in Canada Reviewed", *The Fiddlehead*, 53 (Summer 1962), 61-64.

MIDDLETON, J. K., "Technical Finish Gives a Novel Power to Drive Home a Theme", *Saturday Night*, LXI (September 15, 1945), 21.

MULLINS, S. G., *Culture*, XIX (June 1958), 224-25.

— *Culture*, XX (March 1959), 105-06.

PARKS, M. G., *The Dalhousie Review*, L. (Summer 1970), 285-287.

"Un Recueil de Nouvelles", *Revue de l'Université Laval*, V (October 1950), 171-72.

SANDWELL, B. K., "With 'A Sense of Humility' ", *Saturday Night*, LXVII (April 26, 1952), 32.

SHRIVE, F. W., *Queen's Quarterly*, LXIX (Autumn 1962), 464-65.

"Sketchy Tales", *Saturday Night*, LXXIII (December 6, 1958), 51.

SOMMERHALDER, James, "Any Child", *Alphabet*, 17 (December 6, 1969), 71-72.

SONTHOFF, H. W., "On Ethel Wilson", *Canadian Literature*, 38 (Autumn 1968), 93-94.

STANLEY, Carleton, "Frederick Philip Grove", *The Dalhousie Review*, XXV (January 1946), 433-41.

SWAYZE, Fred, "Dissecting Poets", *Queen's Quarterly*, LXV (Autumn 1958), 534-35.

WEEKES, H. V., *The Dalhousie Review*, XXXIX (Spring 1959), 123, 125.

WILSON, Milton, *The Canadian Forum*, XXXVII (June 1957), 64, 66.

690183